# THE GREEK'S ULTIMATE CONQUEST

BY
KIM LAWRENCE

MILLS & BOON

First Published in Great Britain 2018
by Mills & Boon, an imprint of HarperCollins*Publishers*
1 London Bridge Street, London, SE1 9GF

© 2018 Kim Lawrence

ISBN: 978-0-263-93406-9

MIX
Paper from
responsible sources
FSC® C007454

This book is produced from independently certified FSC™ paper
to ensure responsible forest management.
For more information visit www.harpercollins.co.uk/green.

Printed and bound in Spain
by CPI, Barcelona

# CHAPTER ONE

WHEN HAD HE actually last slept...?

The medication that the medic had administered to him in the field hospital had only taken the edge off his agony and since he'd got on the military air transport to Germany it hadn't even done that, despite the copious amounts of alcohol he'd downed in an attempt to self-medicate.

But now he was finally about to fall sleep, the moment was delayed as a half-burnt log in the open grate disintegrated, sending a star burst of sparks outwards and pulling him back from the brink. He watched through heavy half-closed eyes as the flames flared briefly before fading, leaving dark specks on the sheepskin stretched over the wood floor.

The woman lying across his arm stirred gently before burrowing into his shoulder. He flexed his fingers to relieve the numbness that was creeping into his hand, and with his free hand pushed back a hank of hair tinged silver by the moonlight shining through the open window. He glanced down, the soft light caressing her face revealing the smooth curve of her cheek.

She was, simply, beautiful. It wasn't just the bone structure and the incredible body, but she had something else about her...a *glow*, he decided, smiling at the uncharacteristically sentimental thought as he rubbed a strand of her hair between his fingertips. She was the sort of woman that at any other time in his life he would have gravitated towards. But even though he'd picked her out immediately when she had entered the bar earlier—with a noisy, youthful après-ski group oozing the confidence that came with privilege and intent on having fun and spending money—he had not reacted. Instead shutting out the sound of upper-class voices, he'd turned back to the drink he'd been nursing as he'd sunk once again into his black thoughts.

Then she'd come over to him. Up close she was even more spectacular, and she clearly had the self confidence that went with knowing it as she approached him. A real golden girl complete with golden glow, long gorgeous legs, her lithe body lovingly outlined in tight-fitting ski gear that was suited to her sinuous, athletic body. Her fine-boned face had perfect symmetry, the full lips and the deep blue of her wide-spaced eyes made him think of an angel, a sexy angel with a halo of lint-pale hair that glittered in the reflection of the beaten copper light shade suspended over his table.

'Hello.'

Her voice was low, accentless, and had a slight attractive husk.

A flicker of uncertainty appeared in her eyes when he didn't respond, then after a moment she repeated the greeting, first in French and then Italian.

'English is fine.'

She took the comment as encouragement and slid onto a stool beside him. 'I saw you from...' Without taking her eyes from his face—*they really were the most spectacular eyes*—she nodded towards the group she had arrived with, who seemed to be involved in a noisy shot-down-ing game. The sight of the bunch of spoiled socialites giving the bar staff a hard time twitched his lips into a contemptuous sneer.

'You're missing the fun,' he drawled.

She glanced back at her friends, giving what appeared to be a wince before training eyes that were a shocking shade of blue on him. 'It stopped being fun about two bars ago.' Her soft lips still smiled but a quizzical groove appeared between her brows and her head tilted a little to one side as she continued to stare at him. 'You look...*alone*.'

He gave her a look then, the one that made ninety-nine out of a hundred people back off. The hundredth was generally drunk, although it was obvious this woman wasn't; her blue stare was clear and candid, unnervingly so. Or maybe what unnerved him was the electric charge he could feel in the air between them, a low-level thrum but undeniably present.

'I'm Chloe—'

He cut her off before she could introduce herself fully.

'Sorry, *agape mou*, I'm not good company tonight.' He wanted her to go away, he wanted to be left alone to slide back into the darkness, but when she didn't, he wasn't really sorry.

'Are you Greek?'

'Among other things.'

'So what do I call you?'

Nothing worse than he'd called himself. 'Nik.'

'Just Nik?'

He nodded and after a moment she gave a little shrug of assent. 'Fair enough.'

When her friends had left she had stayed.

This was her room, an apartment in an upmarket chalet—not that they'd made it as far as the bedroom. A trail of their clothing traced their stumbling path from the door to the leather sofa where they lay.

He had always enjoyed the physical, sexual side of his nature but last night… Nik still couldn't quite believe how raw it had been, a true sanity-sapping explosion of need, and for a few moments he had felt free, free of grief, guilt and the oily taint left by the things he had witnessed.

He trailed a hand down her back, letting his fingers rest on the curve of her smooth bottom. As he breathed in her scent he desperately wanted to close his eyes, but for some reason every time he thought about it his glance was drawn across the room to where, he knew, even though the light was too dim to see properly, his phone lay after it had fallen from his pocket.

How did he know it was about to vibrate?

Then it did.

He glanced down to see if the sound had disturbed the sleeping woman and every muscle in his body clenched violently in icy horror and shock, trapping the cry of visceral terror in his throat. He was staring down, not at a warm, beautiful woman, but at the pale, still face of his best friend. The body he held was not warm and breathing but cold and still, the eyes not closed but open and staring up at him, blankly empty!

When he suddenly awoke, gasping, he was not in his bed but beside it on the floor on his knees, shaking like someone in a fever, sweat dripping from his body as he gulped for air. The effort of drawing oxygen into his lungs defined each individual sinew and muscle in his powerful back as he rammed his clenched fists against his rock-hard thighs. The scream that clawed at the edge of his mind remained locked in his raw throat as he struggled to reclaim reality from the lingering wisps of his dreams.

It finally came, and when it did he felt…well, he felt no better or worse than he had on any other of the countless times previously he'd woken out of exactly the same nightmare.

Slowly Nik got to his feet, the normal fluidity of his actions stiff, the athletically honed body so many envied, and even more lusted after, responding sluggishly to commands as he lurched across the room to the bathroom, where he turned on the cold tap of the washbasin full blast and put his head under the stream of cold water.

Fingers curled over the edge of the basin hid the fact he refused to acknowledge, that his hands were shaking, but as he straightened up he was unable to avoid a brief view of his own reflection in the mirror before he turned away, knowing that although the blinding visceral fear was temporarily back in its box, the shadow of it remained in his eyes.

The shower did not entirely banish the shadow either, but it did revive him. He checked the time; four hours' sleep was two hours too little but the idea of returning to bed, probably only to relive the nightmare yet again, held little appeal.

Five minutes later Security buzzed him out of the building, the concierge dipping his head and wishing him a good run when he exited, while privately probably thinking that the guy from the penthouse who regularly took a pre-dawn run was insane. Maybe, Nik reflected grimly as he pulled up the hood of his sweatshirt against the rain, he had a point.

The exercise did the usual trick of clearing his head so by the time, shaved, suited and booted, he skimmed through his emails the night horrors had been banished, or at least unacknowledged. He had other things to focus on, things that were nothing to do with the message on his phone. After noting the caller identity with a grimace, he slid it into his pocket.

He knew without looking at the content that it would be a reminder about the dinner party his sister was hosting that evening, the one he had agreed to attend in a moment of weakness. With Ana it was easier to say yes, because *no* was not a word she understood, neither was single or unattached, at least where her younger brother was concerned.

He slowed as he reached another set of traffic lights that had sprung up overnight, and smothered a sigh as he struggled to push aside the thoughts of his evening entertainment and the inevitable candidate for the position of wife, or at least serious girlfriend material, who would be seated beside him.

He loved his sister, admiring her talent and the fact she juggled a career as a designer with being a single parent. He was ready to admit she had many good traits but unfortunately conceding defeat was not one of them!

Part of his mind on the increasingly heavy traffic he was negotiating, he tried to put the evening ahead out of his mind, but maybe due to his disturbed night the prospect of being polite to one of the perfectly charming women his sister produced on a regular basis to audition for the role of potential mate weighed more heavily on his mind.

He knew that as far as Ana was concerned all his problems would be solved the moment he found a soul mate. He still couldn't decide if she really believed it and though there were occasions when he found her rosy optimism sweet, usually after a bottle of wine, mostly it was intensely irritating.

Hell, if he'd thought love was a cure-all he'd be out looking for it now, but as far as Nik was concerned the search would be in vain. It was a stretch but he was prepared to suspend disbelief and concede that it was possible that there was such a thing as true love, but if this was the case, the way some people were born colourblind, he was love-blind.

It was a disability he was prepared to bear. At least he was never going to be in the position of having to experience the falling *out* of love process. It would be hard to find two people more civilised, more genuinely nice than his sister and her ex, but he had watched their break-up and eventual divorce and it had been toxic! The worst aspect of the split had been the child stuck in the middle. It didn't really matter how hard you tried to protect them from the worst, and they had tried, a kid had to be affected by it.

Give him plain and simple lust any day of the week, and as for growing old alone, surely it was better by far than growing old next to someone you couldn't stand the sight of!

He was prepared to concede that there were happy marriages around but they were the exception rather than the rule.

The car moved five yards before he came to another halt, and someone farther down the line of stationary cars sounded their horn in frustration. Nik raised his eyes heavenwards, the frown lines in his brow smoothing out as his glance landed on the neon-lit face on the advertising billboard across the road.

The advertising agency had clearly gone old school. There was nothing subtle about the message they were sending, just a straightforward fantasy for men to buy into. Use the brand of male face product clutched to the generous bosom of the woman in the bikini and you too would have similarly scantily clad and gorgeous women throwing themselves at you.

*Not this one...* His mobile mouth twitched into a sardonic smile; he was probably one of a handful of people who knew that this particular object of male fantasy was in a secret same-sex relationship. Secret, not because Lucy was concerned about any negative impact on her career, but because of a deal the couple had struck with her partner Clare's soon to be ex-husband. The guy wouldn't contest the divorce if the women waited to go public with their relationship until after he had landed the contract worth multi millions he was in the middle of negotiating with a firm who had built their brand on family values and a squeaky-clean image.

Maybe, Nik mused, if the guy had spent as much time on his marriage as he did on nurturing business deals he might still be married...? After all, if you believed everything you read, maintaining a good relationship took time, energy and hard work. Well, he definitely didn't have the time. As for energy, he was quite prepared to be energetic, but not if the sex seemed like hard work... No, marriage really was not for him.

He was jolted from his reverie by another blast on a horn, from behind him this time. It had a knock-on effect...not *quite* a eureka moment but pretty damn close and, like all good ideas, it was perfectly simple. Actually he couldn't quite figure out why it had not previously occurred to him to counter his sister's relentless matchmaking by turning up with a date of his own choosing and acting like a man in love.

He smiled up at the inspiration for the idea looking down at him...was Lucy Cavendish in town? And if she was, he wondered if the idea would appeal to her sense of humour; failing that he'd appeal to her conscience. After all, she did owe him one as he was the person who'd introduced her to Clare.

The caterers were carrying boxes through the open front door when Chloe arrived. Tatiana had asked her to be early but maybe this was *too* early?

'Go through to the office. Mum's in there.'

Chloe did a double take and realised that one of the caterers holding a box was Eugenie, Tatiana's teenage daughter.

The girl saw her expression and nodded. 'Yeah, I know...not a good look, but Mum insisted I work at least half the holiday to reduce the danger of me being a rich spoilt brat who thinks money grows on trees. You look great!' she added, her eyes widening as she took in the full effect of the sleeveless silk jumpsuit Chloe wore. 'Of course, you have to have legs that go on for ever to get away with it.'

Chloe laughed as the girl whisked away.

The door of the study was open and after a brief tap Chloe went inside. The room was empty except for the dog that was curled up on top of a designer silk jacket that had been flung over a chair. Even crushed and underneath a Labrador the distinctive style of the design made the label it bore unnecessary. *Tatiana* had become famous for her use of bold, brilliant colours and simple wearable designs.

The animal opened one eye and Chloe went over, drawn by a silent canine command. As she stroked his soft ears she looked curiously at the drawings set up on the massive draftsman table that took centre stage in the room.

'Oh, don't look at those. I was having a bad day,' Tatiana exclaimed, walking into the room. In one of her own designs, the petite brunette projected an air of effortless elegance. 'Down, Ulysses!' She gave a little sigh when the dog responded by wagging his tail and staying put. 'Nik says a dog needs to know who's master, but that's the trouble—you already do, don't you, you bad boy?' she crooned.

Chloe gave a smile that she hoped hid the fact that her first thought whenever she heard the name of Tatiana's younger brother was, *Oh, God, not brother Nik again!*

Nothing Tatiana said about her brother challenged Chloe's growing conviction that the man thought he was an expert on everything—and was not shy about sharing his expert opinion.

But then, being reticent and self-effacing were probably not the most obvious characteristics for someone who was the head of a Greek shipping line, and though Chloe knew that Nik Latsis had only stepped into his father's shoes relatively recently, it sounded to her as though they fitted him very well indeed!

Tatiana didn't seem to question or resent the fact that her younger brother had inherited the company simply because he was male, so why should Chloe?

Maybe because she wasn't Greek.

And there was no doubt the Latsis family considered themselves Greek even though they had been London based for thirty years. They were part of a large, well-heeled Greek community that had settled in the British capital. Rich or nouveau riche, they all had the rich part in common, that and being Greek, which seemed to be enough to make them a very tight-knit community where everyone knew everyone and traditions were important.

As she gave the dog one last pat she caught sight of her

reflection in the mirror that made the generously sized room appear even larger, and made a conscious effort to iron out the frown lines that the thought of Tatiana's invisible brother had etched in her forehead.

The invisible part was no accident. It was eighteen months since his father's stroke had brought forward the younger brother's ascension to the 'throne' of Latsis Shipping and he had kept a very low profile, something you couldn't do unless you had loyal family and friends, limitless resources and, she supposed, an inside working knowledge of how the media worked that being an ex-journalist would bring.

*The point being, Chloe,* she told herself sternly, *is that he is invisible. You've never met the guy, and yet here you are making all these judgements on the basis of a few comments and gut instinct.* Something that she'd have been the very first to condemn in anyone else.

'You're being a hypocrite, Chloe.'

The softly voiced self-condemnation caused Tatiana, whose eyes had drifted with a distracted expression to the fabrics pinned on one of the boards, to look up. She directed an enquiring look at Chloe, who shook her head.

'Those colours are beautiful,' Chloe said, nodding to the fabrics, and lifted a finger to touch one piece of silk that was a shade or two deeper than the blue wide-legged jumpsuit she was wearing.

'It would suit you, but I'm not sure...' Tatiana stopped and shook her head. 'Sorry, I just struggle to switch off sometimes.'

She smiled ruefully as she moved to kiss Chloe warmly on her cheek.

'The trials of being artistic,' Chloe teased.

'I don't know about that, but I do know that I am a bit of a workaholic...the work-life, home-life balance always did elude me.' A wistful expression crossed her face. 'Maybe that's why I got divorced...' She shook her dark sleek head slightly and smiled. 'But never mind about that tonight...just look at you!'

Hands resting lightly on Chloe's slim upper arms, she pushed the taller woman back a little. The sombreness of earlier drifted across her face when her glance stilled momentarily on Chloe's legs covered in loose folds of sky-blue silk, but it was gone by the time her eyes reached Chloe's face.

'You look stunning, as usual. I'm not saying it's all about a pretty face, but it definitely helps when you're trying to get men to open their wallets for a good cause... and before you ask you have my permission to put the hard sell on everyone here tonight.'

'People are usually very kind,' Chloe said.

'Especially when they are being guilted into it by the sister of a future queen. But why not use your connections? That's what I always say, and, while I might not have the right sort, your sister certainly does.' She sketched a curtsy and Chloe laughed. Her sister might be a princess and one day destined to be the Queen of Vela Main, but Chloe could not imagine anyone less *royal*. Both sisters had been brought up to believe that what a person did was more important than their title.

'I'll do my very best for the charity,' Tatiana continued in earnest now. 'In my book, I owe you.' She walked across to the mantel where the marble surface was covered with framed photos. She selected one and held it up in invitation for Chloe to see it. 'For what you did for Mel,' she finished, looking fondly at the photo she held.

Chloe shook her head, uncomfortable with the praise. As far as Chloe was concerned, the young Greek girl was her inspiration. 'I didn't do anything.' She took the frame

that Tatiana offered and looked at the photo it held. It was
a snap taken the previous month in a pavement café on a
girls' trip to Barcelona. 'She's a brave girl.'

Chloe had known Tatiana by sight and reputation
before the other woman had boosted Chloe's career by
mentioning her blog in an interview she'd given covering London fashion week, two years ago now, Chloe realised, though it seemed more like a lifetime. Back then
the interview was pretty much responsible for her blog
becoming a profitable overnight success.

Chloe had contacted Tatiana to thank her for the plug
and they had exchanged the odd email but they had never
met in person.

That had happened in a very different context a year
ago, after the designer's god-daughter was moved into
the room next to Chloe's own in the specialist burns unit.
Chloe had already been in there for three months; she'd
known every crack in the ceiling and had been living
vicariously through the love lives of the young nurses
designated to her care.

Though the burns Chloe herself had received in a road
traffic accident had been severe and painful and the healing process long, her own scars were easy to hide from
view under her clothes. But the young woman in the next
room had not been able to hide the damage done to her
face by the fire caused by a gas explosion. Then, as if
life hadn't already thrown enough rubbish at her, the day
after she had arrived at the burns unit her boyfriend had
dumped her, at which point Mel had turned her face to
the wall and announced she didn't want to live.

As she'd listened through the partition wall Chloe's
heart had ached for the other girl. Their first conversation later that night shouted through the wall had been a
one-sided affair, but it had been the first of many.

'You got her through it, Chloe,' Tatiana choked. 'I'll never forget that day I arrived and heard her laugh—you did that.'

'Mel helped me as much as I did her. Did you see the information sheet she put together for me on make-up techniques?' she asked, placing the photo back on the shelf. In doing so she accidentally nudged the one next to it and straightened it, admiring the frame; it was an antique one, the ebony wood delicately carved and rather beautiful.

Chloe was admiring the craftsmanship, running her fingers across the smooth indentations, when her glance drifted across the photo it held. Her mouth tugged into a smile; with a white-knuckle ride in the background, a younger Eugenie smiled back at her, complete with braces, from under the peak of a baseball cap with the logo of an adventure park emblazoned on it.

The jeans-clad man crouched down beside her in the shot was wearing the same cap, and he was… Chloe's smile vanished like smoke as brutal stinging reality hit her like a slap across the face. Pale as paper now, she stared at the male in the picture, wearing jeans, a tee shirt, and a teasing, carefree expression on his handsome face, a face that bore no signs of a tortured soul. There were no shadows that she felt the need to banish; he was just a regular guy…well, only if the *regular* guy in question was more handsome than any man had a right to be with a body that an Olympic swimmer might dream of possessing.

She stood like a statue staring at the photo she held in a hand that quickly developed a visible tremor—the tremor penetrating past the skin level and moving deep inside her.

By sheer force of will she released the breath she was

holding in her lungs, but not the avalanche of questions whirring in dizzying succession through her brain. She felt as though a dozen people were inside her shouting so loudly she couldn't make out the individual questions.

Obviously it couldn't be him but, equally obviously, it was! The man in the photos was the same man who she had spent a never-to-be-forgotten night of lust with. If all learning experiences were as brutal as that one had been, it would not be worth getting out of bed in the morning—happily they weren't and she had moved on.

But that didn't mean she'd forgotten any of it. Forgotten the feelings of emotional hurt and humiliation that had made her physically sick the next morning when she'd realised he'd slipped away during the night. And the worst part was, she had no one to blame but herself. Because she had been the one who had followed her instincts when she'd approached him in that bar, telling herself that what she was doing was somehow meant to be... If they had been handing out awards for naivety and general stupidity that night, she would have walked away with an armful of prizes!

She'd wondered if his name really was Nik. It seemed utterly incredible to her now that she'd ever thought it part of the romantic fantasy element of their night together that she hadn't even known his full name! Time had stripped away the romantic gloss and revealed it for what it truly was—a cheap and tacky one-night stand, even if the sex had been utterly incredible.

Keeping her voice carefully casual, she half turned to Tatiana, as yet unable to tear her eyes from the snapshot. 'How old was Eugenie in this one?'

Tatiana came across and looked at the photo of her daughter and she gave a nostalgic sigh. 'Oh, that was taken on her tenth birthday, although just five minutes afterwards she was throwing up. Nik let her eat a bag of doughnuts then took her on some white-knuckle ride.'

Chloe's own knuckles were bone white where her hand was pressed to her chest. Her poor heart was vibrating against her ribcage, her insides were quivering as she told herself sternly to get a grip, not to mention a sense of proportion. It was only a photo after all, and he was old history.

*Note to self*, she castigated herself, *the next time you decide to make love, don't do it with a complete stranger! No, Chloe, let's be grown up and honest here—it wasn't making love, it was having sex.*

It hadn't been until she'd accepted that particular fact and realised that what they had shared that night had had absolutely nothing to do with a spiritual connection but everything to do with blind lust that she had been able to move on.

*Move on—really? So why was she shaking?*

She put the photo down carefully and smoothed her hands down over the fabric of her jumpsuit. She would not let that man do this to her again; she was not that silly naive girl any longer.

It had been a painful learning experience, but once her pride had stopped stinging and she had stopped feeling basically stupid she'd understood that while empty sex with anonymous strangers could obviously be physically satisfying, it probably wasn't for her. She wasn't exactly holding out for the love of her life, but she did think maybe a bit of mutual respect might be nice.

'So that's your brother Nik,' she said flatly. Sometimes it seemed as if fate had a very warped sense of humour.

Her eyes skimmed the mantel. The same man, she recognised now, was in several of the photos. It wasn't just the time difference that made him look younger, it was the absence of the cynicism and dangerous darkness she had sensed in him that night they'd had sex. What had happened to the man in these photos to turn him into the one she'd met only a few years later?

She dug her teeth into her plump lower lip as she squared her shoulders. Nik Latsis, *her* Nik—it was *so* weird to finally be able to put a full name to the man who had introduced her to sex and the fact it really was the only thing that some men were interested in. Well, his name was actually pretty irrelevant and she couldn't care less what had happened to turn him into such a cold bastard.

Not that she wasn't totally prepared to take her fair share of the blame. After all, 'naive closet romantic meets utter bastard'—it was never going to end well, was it? But she was not that person any more.

'I forgot, you haven't met Nik...have you?' Tatiana asked.

The truth or a lie?

Chloe settled for somewhere in the middle. 'He does look a little familiar...'

*It's the clothes that threw me.*

She brought her lashes down in a concealing sooty curtain and fanned her hot cheeks with a hand, causing the bangles she wore around her wrist to jingle. 'I think summer might finally have arrived,' she commented, ignoring the house's perfect air-conditioning system.

'You might have seen him on the television, perhaps?'

'Television?' A puzzled frown drew Chloe's brows together above her small straight nose. 'I don't think so...' Then it clicked; Tatiana wasn't talking about the present day but her brother's previous life. 'Oh, when you said he was a journalist I thought you meant he was in print...'

His sister nodded. 'He started out in print journalism

but Nik was a war correspondent, and he was on the telly quite a lot actually. He won awards.' Tatiana's pride in her brother's achievements was as obvious as her distress as she enlarged. 'He spent the last two years of his journalistic career embedded with the military, in the worst war zones you can imagine. Nik has always been the sort of person who doesn't do half measures.'

He had certainly been no half-measure lover or, for that matter, halfway callous!

'On his last assignment his cameraman, his best friend, was shot.'

Chloe blanched in shock. 'Did he...?'

Tatiana nodded. 'He died in Nik's arms, but the worst part—at least for the families—was that for three days we knew that there had been a fatality. There were about ten journalists, all from different media outlets pinned down, but we didn't know their identities or who had died.'

Chloe gave an empathetic murmur of sympathy and touched her friend's hand as the older woman closed her eyes and shuddered. 'We all loved Charlie, he had just got engaged...but at the same time we were all so incredibly relieved that it wasn't Nik. It made everyone feel so guilty.'

'Survivor's guilt,' Chloe said, thinking of her sister who, after the accident from which she had escaped unscathed while Chloe had not, had been helped by a therapist. Well, Nik Latsis could afford the best help money could buy.

'You've probably seen him, although professionally he used Mum's maiden name, because he didn't want to be accused of using the family name. Does Kyriakis ring a bell...? Nik Kyriakis?'

Chloe shook her head. 'I've never watched much TV.

There was a rule when we were growing up, half an hour's television a day, and then when I could decide for myself I suppose it had become a habit I never really broke. Even now I listen to the radio rather than switch on the box. It must have been hard for your brother going back to work after what had happened…?'

She had gone back to the spot where the accident had happened—had it been therapeutic? Only in the sense that she had proved to herself that she could do it?

That had been how she had privately charted her recovery: the things she was able to do, the things she could move past—looking at her scars, showing them to her family, getting into a car, driving a car…going back to the winding mountain road where the accident had happened.

'He didn't go back. A day after he returned, our dad had his stroke and couldn't run the company any more; the plan had always been for Nik to step up when the time came.' She stopped, an expression of consternation crossing her face. 'Nik doesn't ever talk about what happened to Charlie, so don't mention it tonight, will you?' she finished anxiously.

If he wanted to bottle things up in a stupid manly way, that was fine by her; she definitely wouldn't be getting him to unburden himself to her. In fact, the idea of seeing him, let alone passing the time of day with him, made the panic gathered like a tight icy ball in her stomach expand uncomfortably.

Ironically there had been a time when she would have paid good money to confront her runaway lover, but that time was long gone; she had no intention of having any sort of conversation with Nik Latsis.

He was history, a mistake, but not one she was going to beat herself up over any more, and one she really didn't want to come face to face with, but, if she absolutely had to, she was going to do it with pride and dignity.

Well, that was the plan anyway.

'I won't,' she promised as the voice in her head reminded her once again that her plans often had a habit of going wrong...

# CHAPTER TWO

'You're late.' Tatiana kissed her brother's lean cheek, grimacing a little as the sprinkling of designer stubble grazed her smooth cheek before one eyebrow rose. She struggled to hide her surprise as she shifted her gaze from her impeccably turned-out brother to the woman who stood with one hand possessively on his dark-suited arm.

'You know Lucy Cavendish?' Placing a hand across her shoulders, he drew the model, her famous dazzling smile firmly in place, close into his side. The redhead tilted her head. Unusually for a woman, in her heels she topped his shoulder.

'I did Tatiana's last catwalk show in Paris. What a lovely home you have.' Lucy's expertly made-up green eyes moved admiringly around the entrance hall with its chandeliers and dramatic staircase.

Tatiana inclined her dark head and delivered an air kiss. 'Thank you. You're looking well, Lucy...' Tatiana looked up at her brother. 'You growing a beard, Nik?'

'With your views on facial hair, Ana, would I dare?'

'Oh, I just *lurve* the moody, broody look.' Lucy's eyes sparkled with teasing amusement as she stroked his cheek, letting her red fingernails slide familiarly over the stubble.

Nik removed the hand firmly from his cheek where it

had lingered and whispered so only she could hear him, 'Don't overdo it, angel.'

As they moved across the hall the sound of voices and laughter drifted out through the open double doors of the drawing room.

'Anyone I know here?' Lucy asked.

'Just a small gathering of friends.'

Letting Lucy go ahead of them, Nik fell into step beside his sister. 'Hope you didn't mind me bringing Lucy.'

'Why should I mind?'

'I thought you might have had me paired off with some good breeding stock...?'

'I don't—' Tatiana stopped and gave a shake of her head, admitting ruefully, 'I suppose I do, but I just want you to be happy and...like you used to be...before...'

Impelled by an inconvenient spasm of guilt, Nik stepped in to hug his sister as suddenly the charade with Lucy seemed less of a good idea. 'I am happy.'

'I like Lucy. Are you two together?'

Nik's glance slid away. She looked so hopeful that, although this had been the idea, he felt reluctant to raise her hopes, knowing full well they were false ones. 'Early days,' he prevaricated slickly.

'I just hope Lucy won't be bored silly,' Tatiana fretted, glancing towards the model who was walking through the double doors. 'It so happens that there is a woman here who might interest you—'

'Just when I thought I might have misjudged you,' he began sardonically.

'Not in that way!' Tatiana cut back. 'She's a good friend of mine.'

'And you wouldn't wish me on a friend?'

She slung him an irritated look. 'I just want you to set a good example when you meet her, and give a *really*

generous donation to the charity—set a good example
for the others.'

'Another of your worthy causes, Ana?'

'This is important to me, Nik.'

'Fine, I'll be generous.'

Chloe glanced at the clock...maybe he was a no show?
Annoyed with herself for caring one way or the other, she
turned her back on the doorway and focused her attention
fully on the man beside her, a middle-aged Greek man
who ran a property development company and seemed
genuinely interested in the charity.

'I admire your enthusiasm but, and I don't want to be
negative, aren't you being a little overambitious? Have
you costed it up properly? The premises alone would—'

'Yes suitable premises, especially here in London,
will be difficult.'

'Which is where I come in?'

Her smile glimmered. 'Your specialist knowledge and
advice would be much appreciated.'

'And my money?' he added shrewdly.

Chloe's dimples appeared. 'I know that Tatiana has already spoken to you about...sorry, I really can't do this.'

The recipient of her half-empty glass of champagne
looked startled and then amused as Chloe popped the
finger food she had been holding into her mouth, swallowed, then smiled. 'That's better!' she said as she held
out her hand for her glass.

Tipping his head, her companion replaced the crystal wine cup in it.

'Mostly I can multitask,' she told him cheerfully. 'I
can do food or drink but not both at the same time. You
wouldn't believe how many outfits I've emptied glasses
of wine down, which makes it sound as though I always

wander round with a glass of pinot in my hand, which I don't.' She delivered another smile. 'I can assure you that your donation will be in sober and sensible hands.'

The older man gave an appreciative chuckle at her tactics. 'Nice try, but I don't recall saying yes.'

Chloe conceded his point with a nod. 'But you didn't say no either and I'm an optimist.'

This time the man's chuckle was loud enough to divert some of the attention currently being given to the model who was making her entrance. 'So let me get this right, you'd like me to let you have the lease on several buildings for a fraction of what they are worth, and what do I get?'

'A warm glow knowing you've done the right thing? Or, failing that, the sort of publicity that money can't buy? The sort of publicity that comes from having your company represent the caring face of capitalism,' Chloe said, thinking wryly that she was getting quite good at this.

The man gave her an approving look tinged for the first time with respect. 'I think we should schedule a meeting, Lady—'

'Call me Chloe,' she cut in quickly.

He tipped his head in acknowledgment of her request. 'Right, Chloe, how about…?'

As the man's eyes moved over her head and his voice trailed away Chloe turned to see what had snatched his attention. The answer was immediately obvious in the shape of a glamorous redhead in a glittering gown more suited to a red carpet event than a dinner party.

Immediately tolerant of her companion's distraction, she turned to study the new arrival with some curiosity. In her experience people you had only previously seen beautifully lit on the screen or airbrushed in magazines rarely lived up to expectations, but Lucy Cavendish did and then some.

She looked beyond her hostess and the model to see if Lucy had come with someone. The woman's past boyfriends had included not one but two Hollywood A-listers, a Russian oligarch and the heir to a banking fortune, so Chloe was expecting a handsome face or serious money, someone who might be interested in donating to a good cause, perhaps?

She got neither...or rather actually what she got was both!

What she also got when she saw that Lucy's date was Nik was a jolt similar to the occasion her hairdryer had given her an electric shock, times a hundred. A home-made and dangerously uncontrolled defibrillation that felt as if a hammer had landed on her chest and made her limbs feel weak.

But this was fine; she could totally deal with it...

*Not dealing with it, Chloe!*

Ignoring the mocking voice in her head, she took a deep breath, straightened her slender square shoulders, cleared her throat and readjusted the chunky necklace of raw amethyst slices that hid the pulse pounding at the base of her throat.

*Breathe*...she told herself, so she did, and for good measure she focused on the positive.

The worst was over and, as *worsts* went, seeing the man you'd made the mistake of sleeping with without knowing his full name was, on the scale of things, pretty low-key. A couple of minutes and her nervous system would catch up with the message and by tomorrow she'd be laughing—all right, maybe *smiling* about it.

But that was tomorrow; being realistic today, as in the

next sixty seconds, she was aiming for a less ambitious goal. Her legs stopping shaking would be a good start.

She stifled a stab of impatience; her nervous system was getting this situation way out of proportion. After all, what was the worst that could happen?

And what was the worst anyway: him remembering her or him not?

Her mobile lips quirked into a smile as she considered the alternatives. An awkward reunion or a hit to her ego?

Did it really matter?

The fact that she could even ask herself the question was a sign of how much she'd changed in a little over a year. There had been a time when, despite the outward confidence she projected, what people thought about her had mattered, and she wanted the right people to like her...she wanted to fit in.

The journey to where she was today had not been easy, but everything had changed. Well, maybe not *everything*, she conceded, watching the new arrival above the rim of the glass she raised to her lips. Still, even at a distance, he had the ability to make the muscles deep in her pelvis quiver...so it was lucky she could consider this phenomenon in an objective way, wasn't it?

She might not be able to achieve total physical indifference to the male magnetism he oozed, but she was more than a bundle of hormones...despite the fact that he was, she thought, studying him through the protective sweep of her lashes, just as incredible-looking as she remembered.

They said you always remembered your first and it turned out they were right. The self-mocking glint in her wide-spaced sky-blue eyes faded and a tiny pucker appeared between her darkly defined feathery brows as she realised how intact her memory of him was, not just the

way he looked, or moved, but the texture of his skin…
the smell of his… She took a shaky breath and straightened her shoulders, slamming the door on that particular
memory. *It was just a lapse of judgement, ancient history, Chloe,* she told herself. *Do not revisit.*

'What a stunning woman!'

Chloe started slightly at her companion's comment and
tore her eyes from the tall figure whose dominant presence had made her forget about the woman he'd brought
with him, although they made a pretty magnificent couple. 'Yes, she is.' Stunning was probably an understate-
ment.

'But I'd say she's high maintenance, and I can't see
her climbing Kilimanjaro.

The comment startled a laugh from Chloe. 'It sounds
to me like you measure all women by some pretty high
standards.'

He smiled and nodded. 'My wife is an extraordinary
woman.'

Chloe stood and listened as the man launched into
what was clearly his favourite subject. An emotional
lump settled in her throat as he talked about his wife.
What would it feel like to be the centre of a man's uni-
verse? she wondered wistfully.

Nik walked past his sister and moved to where Lucy
stood.

'Maybe this isn't such a good idea,' he muttered.

'I was the one who told you that,' the model reminded
him. 'But you've been my beard on more than one occasion, darling, so I kind of owe you. Do you realise how
much money is in this room tonight?'

His eyes moved over the heads of the fellow guests
assembled; most were members of the Greek expat com-

munity, and all of them would have considered not having a private yacht as being poverty-stricken. 'That figures. Ana is raising money for one of her causes again.'

'So you're not in danger of meeting Ms Right here. Does that mean you're dumping me already, darling?'

'Funny... God, I need a drink.'

He placed a guiding hand under Lucy's elbow, and she immediately exclaimed mockingly, 'Ooh, darling, I do so love it when you're masterful. Ah!'

She staggered a little as Nik suddenly released her arm without warning.

It was an automatic response to a soft peal of laughter that made Nik turn his head. Although it hadn't been loud, there was something attractively infectious about the sound that tugged his lips into a smile.

As his eyes surfed across the heads of the other guests to the source of the sound, his smile snuffed out as recognition crashed through his nervous system like a tsunami, and for several seconds his mind went a total blank, the effect of sheer shock colliding with serendipity.

He took a deep breath and decided he'd call it something more mundane—*convenient*. Or he would once he got his rampant, raging libido under control. It took another few deep breaths to think beyond the heat that had streaked down his body and settled painfully in his groin.

His cognitive powers were clearly working on the reserve battery. He had no idea how long he stood there paralyzed, it could have been a second or an hour, before, like a man waking from a trance, he finally shook his head.

The air trapped in his lungs hissed out as in a single urgent sweep his dark, penetrating stare took in every single detail of her. The soft shiny blonde hair falling from a slight widow's peak down her back and cut shorter at the sides to frame a vivid beautiful face, the sinuous curves of her lush body outlined by the flowing lines of blue silk.

She was stunning.

He'd sometimes wondered, generally around two a.m., if he exorcised the woman, would he finally exorcise the nightmare? The two seemed so intrinsically linked, maybe they were interdependent? It had been an intellectual exercise he'd never really taken seriously as he hadn't expected their paths to cross again.

Well, it was no longer intellectual, and neither was the roar in his blood, and he knew that not to explore the theory now that he had the opportunity would be insane!

Chloe knew Nik was standing there even before Spiros's glance moved past her, alerted by the fine invisible downy hairs on her body rising in reaction to his invisible presence.

She emptied her glass carefully, wiped her expression of anything that could be interpreted as a desire to dig a big hole and jump in it and mentally circled the wagons against attack.

If she refused to be defined by the scars she wore, she was definitely not going to be defined by a past mistake, even if he was six foot three and sinfully gorgeous!

Her defensive stance wasn't against anything he might say or do, as there was a very strong possibility that he wouldn't even remember the night they had spent together, but against her own indiscriminate hormones, which still, it seemed, responded independently of her intellect to his rampant animal magnetism.

*Oh, for God's sake, Chloe, you need to get a life!*

While she was silently chastising herself Nik had moved level with her. 'Spiros.'

His voice had the same rough velvet, almost tactile quality she remembered…but this time she was only shivering because she was standing in a draft, she told herself stubbornly.

They were actually standing level, side by side as he stretched out a hand to the older man, but Chloe didn't turn her head. She didn't need to, because she could already feel the sheer physical power of his tall, muscled frame.

'No Petra tonight?'

'No, she's resting up. She sprained an ankle during training.'

Nik made a sympathetic noise in his throat. 'For *another* marathon?'

The older man gave a rueful nod. 'I think it's addictive.'

'You not going to join her?'

'I know my limitations.' Chloe, who felt as though her *casual* social expression could do with some work but needed all her focus to control her too rapid breathing, took encouragement from the fact that Spiros didn't seem to notice anything amiss as he touched her arm and looked at Nik. She was still working her way up to it. 'Do you know Chloe?'

She held her breath.

'Of course; we go way back,' Nik said smoothly.

'Royal connections—you kept that quiet, Nik.'

No longer able to delay the moment, Chloe turned her head, her features arranged in a smile that was intended to project polite indifference, although she had a horrible feeling that a touch of the hunted animal had crept in!

Her first hope had been that he wouldn't remember her; the second was that up close he would have some flaw she had forgotten, but again her fairy godmother had not granted her wish.

So Plan B it was, then: be polite, be distant, be… Oh, God, on an intellectual level the dark, predatory, raw animal magnetism stuff did nothing for her, only it seemed the message hadn't filtered through to the non-intellectual parts of her that were only listening to the hormonal clamour—but then it was pretty loud.

His male beauty, and beauty was no exaggeration, hit her at a purely visceral level. She had never experienced anything like it before—well, just the once.

His high knife-sharp cheekbones, strong aquiline nose, and angular jaw even dusted with stubble gave his face a patrician cast, though this was offset by the overtly sensual outline of his mobile mouth, twisted at that moment into a faintly cynical smile. The same emotion was reflected in his eyes, his quite simply spectacular eyes; deep set and heavy lidded, and fringed with dense, straight, spiky lashes, they were a stunning dark chocolate brown.

Pinned by those dark eyes, she experienced a 'rabbit in the headlight' moment and froze.

'How are you… *Chloe*?' He seemed to roll the word over his tongue as though he were tasting it.

As *he'd tasted her*… Chloe pushed the thought away but not before her body's core temperature had raised a few uncomfortable degrees. She lifted a hand to her neck to feel the dull vibration of her heavy pulse, and she fingered the uncut gemstones that felt cold compared to her skin.

From somewhere she manufactured a smile but the effort made her cheek muscles ache while she silently struggled to keep the door locked against forbidden memories. It wasn't about wanting to forget him, she thought, but more not wanting to remember and be reminded of the things she strongly suspected she might never experience again.

And maybe that was a good thing, she rationalised. Yes, head-banging, uninhibited sex was good—it was pretty excellent—but so was waking up with someone who actually cared for you, or for that matter was physically still there in the morning.

Refusing to acknowledge the sense of loss that still lay like a heavy weight in her chest, she reminded herself that she was looking, or she would be when the time came, for more in a man than his knowledge of the female anatomy... Hell, clumsy with feeling was infinitely preferable to the refined torture of a skilled touch with no emotion behind it.

'How long has it been?' he asked coolly.

'I'm not sure,' she lied, thinking, *Eighteen months, eight days and thirty-one minutes...not that I'm counting.*

She stiffened when without warning he bent his head and brushed her mouth lightly with his. His lips were warm, reminding her of when they had been even warmer, when he had tasted of her... The muscles low on her pelvis cramped as she stood as still as a statue, fighting with all her might the shameful urge to lean in and kiss him back.

The gasp she locked in her throat ached as she breathed in the warm male scent of him through flared nostrils.

It wasn't until he lifted his head that she realised she was holding his sleeve, though she had no memory of grabbing it. Disturbing, but there was no point reading too much into it, she decided as she let it casually fall away, ignoring the tingling sensation in her fingertips.

Nik smiled. The quiver he'd felt run through her body as he'd kissed her reminded him of just how receptive she'd been that night...how *giving* she'd been. And he'd taken... He countered the irrational slug of guilt with a reminder that she was the one who had taken the initiative that night, she'd made all the running and she hadn't acted like a woman who would take no for an answer.

His smile, the glimmer of dark danger glittering deep in his eyes, elicited an involuntary spasm of excitement in her belly that made Chloe feel ashamed.

'You look well.' She looked incredible, though up close there was less of the outdoorsy golden glow he remembered. Her skin was creamy, the faint touch of colour in her cheeks highlighting the smooth contours, the freckles along her cheekbones paler too, but she was, if anything, even more delicious than he remembered.

'Thank you, and how are you—sorry, Nik, wasn't it?'

The composed words aimed somewhere close to his left ear were prim, but the message shining in her deep cobalt-blue eyes as they glittered up at him was neither prim nor polite.

They said quite clearly, *Go to hell!*

Her reaction threw him off his stride, in the same way he realised he'd have been thrown if he'd reread a favourite book and found a main character had suddenly been given a different personality.

Except the woman in his dreams had never had a personality beyond being warm, giving, passionate and available when he had needed her, and he had not been curious about what lay beyond those qualities.

Realising that there *was* a beyond came with a sense of shock as Nik struggled to consider her negative reaction to him dispassionately, but got sidetracked by his own reaction to her.

The problem being there was very little room left for dispassion after the explosive blast of primal desire that obliterated everything else when he looked at her. It was like walking...no, *running* full pelt into a ten-foot wall of lust.

The time it took his stupefied brain to push past this fresh blast of raw hunger was only moments but it felt longer, and the mere fact that he *had* to make the effort deepened the frown lines in Nik's broad forehead.

In his previous life, he had cultivated dispassion until it required no effort, and it was second nature. He'd seen men and women in his old line of work who hadn't managed to do that, and the personal toll it had taken on them had not been good to see. You needed to be able to keep an emotional distance.

He had witnessed acts of bravery and self-sacrifice that were humbling, but for every one of those inspiring acts there were a hundred acts and images of suffering and inhumanity. You carried those nightmare images around with you and they ate you from the inside.

The sheer absurdity of comparing a war zone to a dinner party where people were toting glasses of wine instead of automatic weapons almost dredged up a smile. *Almost.*

# CHAPTER THREE

'I'm—'

'With Lucy Cavendish...' Chloe paused, head tilted in challenge, to let the reminder sink in and had the satisfaction of seeing an expression of shock chase across his handsome face.

'Lucy...hell, I forgot about her!' A quick glance located the model, who was deep in conversation with another guest. Nik dragged a hand across his hair-roughened jaw in annoyance; he must have left her standing there looking like... He gritted out a curse. 'I'm never going to hear the end of this.'

The wrathful, choking gasp of sheer disbelief that escaped Chloe's lips drew his attention back to her face.

If there had been even the *faintest* suggestion of guilt in his reaction, she thought it would have gone some way to redeeming him...actually, no, it wouldn't!

Wanting to make excuses for him made her even angrier—as if there could be any excuse for a man who arrived with one woman and then came on to another with all the subtlety of a sledgehammer!

It made her wonder whose bed he had walked straight into after being in hers.

There had been a time when the thought would have hurt...now it simply made her stomach quiver queasily.

'It's so inconsiderate of a woman to expect you to re-member that you came with her.' She produced a saccha-rine-sweet sympathetic smile, waiting until he frowned slightly in response to her comment before slinging out sarcastically, 'I suppose she even expects you to be there when she wakes up in the morning.'

The words hung there, every syllable oozing with ex-actly the sort of subtext Chloe had wanted to avoid. She sounded just like what she hated most: a victim.

Someone to pity.

Her narrow-eyed glare dared him to show it, but, al-though her comment had surprised a flicker of reaction, it was something else she saw move at the backs of his eyes. Fine, she could deal with something else, actually *anything* else, but *pity*.

'You were asleep.' This was the reason he avoided one-night stands; there was the potential for the stranger you went to bed with assuming that one night of sex con-nected you in some deep and meaningful way.

'I'm not talking about me.' She lifted her feathery brows in an attitude of mild surprise that he should think otherwise, then, willing herself not to blush, she pro-nounced bluntly, 'We had sex but we were not in a re-lationship. Although it would have been useful if you had woken me as I had somewhere I needed to be.' She wrinkled her brow, giving the impression she was try-ing to recall the sequence of events—events that couldn't have been more indelibly imprinted on her had someone branded them into her soul. 'I'm pretty sure I was late.' In her head she clutched the invisible award to her chest as a voice pronounced, *And the award for most convinc-ing liar goes to... Chloe Summerville!*

The dream had once more become a nightmare be-fore he'd ever reached the moment where he'd made the choice to leave her sleeping, not that waking her had ever really been an option. Good manners versus getting to his dying father's bedside after receiving the call about his stroke had been a no brainer.

And yes, he'd been relieved not to have to speak to her again.

Relieved to avoid the potential morning-after awkwardness and recriminations. It hadn't been his first one-night stand, but those other encounters had all been with fellow journalists, and there had been some mutual respect on a professional level between him and the smart, independent women who had shared his bunk. There had been no need to explain the desire he had felt to escape the sights and sounds of war for a few hours and let passion drown it all out. The connections had been brief, pleasurable, but nothing deeper remained.

He wouldn't have cared if any of them had forgotten his name, or implied that the memory they'd walked away with after sleeping with him was that they'd had somewhere else to be but had overslept! His ego took a few startled seconds to recover from the blow while recognising the irrationality of his reaction. Chloe Summerville's cool attitude was *exactly* what he looked for in women he gravitated towards. Women who had a male approach to sex; women who did not expect or even welcome sentiment in their liaisons, but enjoyed sex in an uncluttered and simple way.

'Sorry, I had someplace I needed to be too…but unlike you I wasn't too late.'

His father's prognosis had been grim. The doctors had been all for calling time and letting nature take its inevitable and cruel course, but his mother had insisted they try a third lot of clot-busting drugs. When Nik had walked into the room, his father had been sitting up with nothing but a slight hesitation in his speech to show he'd even had a stroke and people had been talking about miracles.

'Well, it's…nice to see you again, lovely to catch up…' Chloe said absently, adopting the tone you used when you bumped into someone whose name you kept forgetting. 'But if you'll excuse me, tonight is about work and I need to circulate.' Giving her best impression of a woman with her priorities firmly sorted, she flashed him a generic smile and turned back towards where Spiros stood talking to a small group of guests.

Even if he'd taken everything else out of the equation the dismissal would have awoken his interest, if only for the fact that it was new territory for Nik. Women did not usually walk away from him. His curiosity overcame his irritation… So, all right, it was something a lot stronger than irritation, but he didn't need to waste energy trying to identify it as it morphed seamlessly into the much easier to deal with lust and his eyes became riveted on her long, sinuous curves and the gentle sway of her hips.

If sleeping with her again was the way to finally lay his nightmares to rest, great. If not, the trying was going to be fun. Not trying at all had stopped being a possibility the second he'd set eyes on her.

The frustration raging through his veins made it hard for him to formulate a plan of action, as there had been no plan required in his dreams. On a conservative estimate he'd been making love to Chloe every other night for the past year…except this wasn't a dream, it—*she*—was the real deal! And Chloe Summerville was *more* in every way than the woman he remembered. A halfwit could have worked that out in thirty seconds.

And Nik was accounted to be quite intelligent.

She had been pulled into a group several feet away

from where he stood alone, and he watched like a hawk as she lowered her lashes over a smile in response to something Spiros had said. In profile he could see the little quiver of the fine muscles in her throat and along the delicate line of her jaw, and he wondered why he found it so fascinating.

Was he finally losing his mind?

Chloe's legs were still shaking but, as there was no longer any imminent possibility they would give out beneath her, she let go of the image of herself lying on the floor and people staring down at her. Sad, they'd say, she used to be able to stand on her own two feet... She suddenly realised a moment too late to avoid awkwardness that the extended silence was one she was meant to fill. Chloe gave an apologetic smile.

'Sorry. I wasn't following; I was just trying to remember if I put an aspirin in my bag.' She delved into the limited depths of her bag, her hair falling in a concealing curtain around her face.

Still she couldn't quite escape the conversation replaying in her head... When he had asked her how long it had been since they'd met, she'd had a nasty shock. Up to that point she hadn't known that she knew the answer even to the day and hour, but she clearly did... God, but it was terminally depressing.

What, she asked herself, had she ever seen in him?

Beyond of course the face, the body, the high-voltage charge of raw, scalp-tingling sensuality he had oozed... Beyond that, nothing at all!

Other than the dark brooding aura tinged with danger and a touch of vulnerability.

Well, he wasn't vulnerable now and she was no longer the romantic little fool she had been, but, considering her reaction to Nik just now, it was lucky that she had decided celibacy was the way to go... Not for ever—just short term. Who knew what the future held?

But one of the advantages of celibacy was that she could stand here now and look at this incredibly...really incredibly sexy man, and remember, in a way that sort of felt as if it had happened to someone else, how it had felt to have his warm, no, *hot* flesh slide over hers and it wasn't a problem.

*God, you are such a liar, Chloe Summerville.*

In fact, if she had truly believed she was cut out for celibacy long term, it would have simplified life in general, she concluded, studiedly ignoring the scornful voice in her head.

'You have a headache?' a woman whose name Chloe couldn't recall, despite being normally good about that sort of thing, asked.

'It's not that bad.'

Then Nik touched her arm. She knew it was him without even looking at his long fingers brown against her skin, and suddenly it was *extremely* bad. The thump, thump in her temples was keeping time with her heartbeat as Chloe felt a primitive thrill run along her nerve endings. Deeply ashamed, she waited for the fluttering inside her to subside and, under cover of looking in her bag again, calmed her breathing.

'Lost something?' he asked.

'Just an aspirin; I'm getting a headache.' *And I'm looking at it.* But she wasn't. She looked everywhere but at the tall dynamic figure towering over her, which was not something that happened often when you were five feet ten.

Eyes she had control over, but not her thoughts that drifted back to the moment she had first seen him, as if she were stuck in some sort of mind-destroying time loop. The last thing she had anticipated when they had crowded into the almost empty bar was that she would leave with a total stranger. She'd never been a person who was led by her hormones and, while she'd had any number of male friends, she'd not had a lover.

She had dated, obviously, but things had usually ended in an *it's me not you* sort of way. And she had started to think it was—that she was simply one of those women who weren't highly sexed.

Until that night.

Whatever had been lying dormant within her had surfaced with a vengeance!

'Oh, Chloe, have you met Olivia?' Spiros asked, oblivious to any atmosphere, drawing a striking middle-aged woman into the group.

Chloe shook her head, welcoming the opportunity to turn her back on the biggest mistake of her life to this point.

'Olivia, this is the young woman I was telling you about. Olivia was very interested when I told her about your project; her husband, who isn't here tonight, is a plastic surgeon.'

Chloe beamed. 'That's why you look familiar!' she exclaimed. 'I've seen the photo of you that your husband has on his desk at work.'

Listening to her, Nik twisted his lips in a cynical smile. The plastic surgeon must be very good at his job because you really couldn't tell Chloe had had any work done at all. Whatever it had been, he decided, watching her expressive face as she chatted with animation to the older woman, it hadn't been Botox.

Though now he thought about it there were changes, though not those he associated with surgical intervention. Some of the youthful softness he remembered in her face had gone, had become more *refined*, revealing a breathtaking bone structure. As he continued to study her the therapeutic benefits having sex with her might bring to him slid to the back of his mind, leaving having sex with her as soon as possible just because he wanted to very much in the forefront.

'So sorry,' he interjected.

This time with the touch of his cool hand on her wrist Chloe couldn't stop herself turning towards him; the intention was defensive, the result was not!

He was standing very close to her and she stiffened, her chest lifting as she took a deep breath and held it while, inside her ribcage, her heart rate climbed like that of an athlete waiting for the starter's pistol.

Fighting the impulse to cover her mouth with her hand as his eyes drifted to her lips and stayed there, she waited until he had stepped back far enough for her to escape the heat from his body to release the air trapped in her lungs, but unfortunately his aura of sexuality had a wider radius.

'You don't mind if I steal Chloe, do you?' he asked, taking her elbow. To an observer his attitude as much as his body language was suggestive of a long and intimate relationship with her.

The suggestion might have drawn a smile from her if her facial muscles were not locked in what she sincerely hoped was an expression of indifference. What they had shared had been little more than a collision! Granted, an extremely *intimate* collision... As a series of freeze-frame images flashed through her head they had an almost out-of-body quality to them.

She had fallen asleep in his arms, and as she'd drifted off she'd found herself thinking that she had never felt more comfortable with anyone in her life.

Comfortable was something she didn't feel right now as he half dragged her across the room; if she could, she would happily have crawled out of her skin. But pulling away would have made her look even more conspicuous.

He came to a halt in one of the deep window embrasures where the half-drawn curtains gave it an element of privacy that Chloe could have done without.

She immediately pulled away, retreating as far as physically possible. He countered her action by raising one sardonic brow.

Chloe embraced the anger that prickled through her with something approaching relief, while simultaneously ignoring the worrying excitement that popped like champagne bubbles in her bloodstream, making her feel light-headed, which probably made the little head toss with attitude she gave a mistake, but she did it anyway.

'What the hell do you think you are you doing?' she muttered under her breath.

The silky fair hair that streamed down her slender back settled into attractive waves around her face. As he watched the process he suddenly remembered it had taken a long time to gather it all up in his hand and each time his fingers had brushed her skin she had shivered.

*Good question, Nik.* What the hell was he doing?

He said the first thing that came into his head. 'So you're a royal of where?'

'Do you mind? I was having an important conversation back there!'

He shrugged his magnificent shoulders. 'So have a conversation with me.' *So I can look at you.* 'And if by important you mean you were about to get a donation for whatever charity it is… I'll double it,' he said casually.

She expelled a hissing sigh. 'Am I meant to be impressed by your altruism, seeing as you don't even know what the money is for?'

'Does it matter?'

She gritted her teeth and fought the impulse to slap him—anything that would break through his armour of sheer selfishness.

'Clearly not to you!' she countered contemptuously.

'You still haven't told me...'

'Told you what?'

'Royal how?'

She gave a growling sound of aggravation through her clenched teeth. 'My family,' she said finally in a bored, reading-the-telephone-directory voice, 'lives on East Vela; it's an island.' Most people didn't have a clue where it was, though most had watched the recent royal wedding on the television.

Nik proved a little more informed.

'The Vela that has just been reunified.'

She nodded.

'So where do you fit in?'

Chloe used her stock reply. 'I'm the sister who hasn't married the future King.'

'Lucky you.'

It was not the usual stock response and Chloe bristled defensively at the slightest suggestion of criticism of her brother-in-law. 'Lucky me? Most people envy my sister!'

'Do you?' The speed with which she had jumped to the man's defence made him wonder if there wasn't a personal element to her reaction, and the possibility tugged his lips into a cynical sneer.

The sheer unexpectedness of his response made Chloe blink and shake her head. 'What sort of question is that?'

He ignored the spiky question and reverted to his original comment. 'I meant lucky because a queen with any kind of history has to be a nightmare for the PR people-lovers with kiss-and-tell stories coming out of the wood-work,' he explained, pointing out the obvious.

She was tempted, but only for a moment, to retort that her *only* lover was more concerned about keeping a low profile than she was, so that was problem solved. But what would he say if he knew that? The question circling in her head jolted her back to her usual common-sense mode.

Unable to adopt a sufficiently *shallow socialite* tone while she was looking at the outline of his disturbingly sensual mouth, Chloe switched her focus to his hard, stubble-covered jaw. 'Yeah, it really was a lucky escape for me,' she began, and then stopped, her eyes darkening as the memories of feeling cheap and used, still fresh and raw, surfaced once again. Why was she pretending to be someone she wasn't? She didn't care what he thought of her and her chin lifted a notch in defiance. 'Oh, why don't you just call me an easy lay and have done with it?'

His half-closed eyes lifted from the heaving contours of her breasts and collided with her blue shimmering glare. She pulled in a deep breath and, lower lip caught between her white teeth, took a moment to control the quiver in her voice before she drove home her point.

'Just because you treated me with zero respect, Nik, do not assume that I don't respect myself!'

She was lecturing him! Nik was too astonished to immediately react to her accusation and too ashamed to admit anywhere but in the privacy of his own thoughts that he probably deserved it.

'And for the record this is the twenty-first century; no-body expects a prince to marry a virgin bride these days!'

'Again, that's lucky or the European royalty would be a doomed species...' As he spoke the gaps between his words extended as he almost lost track of what he was saying. Her currently outraged attitude meshed with the images and little snatches of memory from that night in his head, flickering faster and faster until he could hear his own thoughts from back then—*so deliciously tight*, so *excitingly shocked...* As if everything *was* new to her, shockingly new! Had she been a virgin?

'We are a doomed species anyway, I suspect,' she was saying. 'They call it evolution, but I suppose royals are a bit like dinosaurs. In the future there will be entire floors of museums displaying our fossilised remains in glass cases.'

'Evolution is preferable to revolution... How didn't I treat you with respect?' he suddenly shot at her, trying to catch her by surprise so she would answer him truthfully.

She said nothing.

'So you *did* have a problem with me walking out on you?'

Her eyelids half lowered. 'It was a first for me, I admit.'

A first? A first of what, exactly? The idea that she could have been a virgin, considering the way she'd approached him that night, was totally crazy, and even if it were true, did he actually want to know? Didn't he have enough guilt in his life without adding any more? The problem was that now the idea was out there, swimming around in his brain, he had to voice it, even if he did end up looking like a fool.

'The first time you'd woken up with the pillow beside you empty, or the first time for you full stop?'

She felt a trickle of sweat trace a sticky path down her back and decided to deliberately misunderstand him. 'First one-night stand? You really haven't read any of the surveys in the magazines, have you? Everyone's doing it.'

'The thing about those surveys is that people lie.'

His intent stare made her feel as though he were look-ing directly into her head and she could feel the blush she was willing away materialise until she felt as though every inch of her skin were on fire.

'And I'm not talking about one-night stands,' he added flatly.

Pushed into a corner, she reacted with cool-eyed hau-teur. 'I really don't think there's any need for a post-mor-tem...but if you're asking what I think you're asking, I don't think I owe you any explanation.'

'So you *were* a virgin.'

'Weren't we all once...even you?' Hard as it was to imagine. 'How old were...?' Her eyes flew wide. 'Oh, God, I said that out loud, didn't I?'

'I was sixteen and she was...older.' The glamorous, bored stepmother of one of his friends at boarding school, and he'd been very willing to be seduced. 'But even at sixteen I would not have thought it the greatest idea in the world to pick up a total stranger in a bar and have sex with them.'

'It wasn't exactly planned!'

'Look, I'm fine with youthful rebellion. I've been there and done that, but I sure as hell don't much like being the unwitting partner of it.'

Chloe felt her embarrassment slip away, incredulous anger rushing in to fill the vacuum; his hypocrisy was staggering. 'So now you're the victim and *I* should apolo-gise? Not that there is a victim, I mean... I just saw you that night and...' She met his eyes and looked away. 'Oh, for heaven's sake, it's not as though you were fighting me off with a stick, is it?'

A laugh was wrenched from Nik's throat before he closed his eyes and wondered how a man could feel like a defiler of innocence and incredibly turned on at the same time.

'I guess I crushed a few of your romantic illusions,' he said heavily.

She sucked in a deep breath. 'Well, it had to happen sometime so relax; after the therapy I'm totally fine.' She stopped suddenly, remembering that she was talking to someone who might really have needed therapy for something more than making a poor choice. She'd slept with the wrong man; he'd seen his friend die in his arms. 'Not that there is anything funny about therapy...in fact, it's a very useful tool,' she told him earnestly.

A nerve began to slowly clench and unclench in Nik's jaw, and it had a mesmeric effect on Chloe.

'What has my sister been saying to you about me?'

Chloe began to shake her head, thinking his sister's opinion of him proved that love really *was* blind... *Lust*, however, was a completely different proposition... She tilted her chin and refused to acknowledge the shameful ache of arousal she felt just looking at him, but in her own defence this man took the term eye candy to a whole new level! 'Absolutely nothing...except of course that you are an expert on just about everything. To be totally honest with you, I'd got sick and tired of hearing the sound of your name.'

All the time she had been ripping up at him he'd stood there looking at her in that disturbing way. When she finally stopped talking he placed a finger against her lips just to make sure he was not interrupted. 'You are really, truly *perfect*! Hell, I so want to take you to bed right now.'

The raw driven declaration, barely more than a husky whisper, made her catch her breath, the air between them shimmering with suppressed sexual tension. She could only stand there, her eyes wide as he moved his finger down her cheek, the light touch, barely there, making her shiver with delicious sensation.

Her eyes had half closed in drugged pleasure when from somewhere a sliver of sanity shattered the sensual haze.

*What the hell are you doing, Chloe?*

'Does that line really work for you?' She was pretty sure it did, and she'd have been yet another of the women who'd fallen for it if it hadn't been for that one word... *perfect*! He still saw her as the woman with the perfect body he remembered from eighteen months ago.

The ugly reality would surely have him running for the hills.

'It isn't a line.' His heavy-lidded eyes moved in a slow approving sweep from the top of her glossy head to her feet in kitten-heeled slingbacks. 'You look fantastic.'

'Yes, I know.' But *looks*, she reminded herself, were cruelly deceptive. Even if she had been tempted to accept the offer he was making, she knew that it wasn't about her; it was only the perfect body that he wanted.

The body that no longer existed.

Loss was something she didn't normally allow herself to feel but it slammed through her now.

'I'd forgotten how direct you were. It's really refreshing,' he said.

The memory of how direct she'd been brought a flush to her face. If she ever regained the sort of confidence she'd once had, then it wouldn't be with a man like Nik Latsis. It would be with a man who could see beyond her scars, and who would want her for the woman she really was.

'Ah, well, I'm so glad to have refreshed you, and speaking of which, if you'll excuse me, I'm going to refresh my glass. I'm not interested—is that direct enough for you?'

'I'd be devastated if I believed you,' he returned with a level look.

'Believe me, you are the *last* man in the world I would be interested in!' Interested, no, she was *fascinated*...but equally she recognised it was an unhealthy 'moth to the flame' sort of fascination. One that would only lead to her being burnt up, and not in a good way.

'Never mind, Nik. If I was interested you'd be the first man to know...or maybe the second,' Lucy Cavendish corrected. 'My dentist has the loveliest eyes.' Her smile deepened as she looked at Chloe. 'So have you.'

Chloe's face burned with embarrassed heat.

Just how long had the model been standing there listening to them? And yet she didn't seem even a jot put out by what she'd heard... Maybe because she had heard it all before? Chloe speculated. Maybe she was fine with sharing her man? Or even...? *None of my business,* she told herself, swiftly closing down this lurid avenue of speculation.

'Dinner is served and I'm starving,' Lucy drawled, then, turning to Chloe, she added, 'I loved your blog, by the way. If you want to know any of the dirty details on this one, I'm the girl to come to.' She gave her a conspiratorial wink before leading Nik away.

# CHAPTER FOUR

Dazed and bewildered, Chloe experienced a quite irrational sense of abandonment as she watched the couple walk away arm in arm. She hung back as the guests
made their way through the double doors, which had
been flung open revealing a long table covered in white
linen and groaning with antique crystal and fine china.
The last to enter the room, Chloe saw that Eugenie was
directing guests to their places. As she watched Nik bent
down and kissed his niece's cheek.

'I'm working, Uncle Nik,' she remonstrated, kissing
him back despite her protest.

Chloe watched him throw a quizzical glance at his
sister. 'Child labour, Ana?'

'Laying the foundations for a healthy work ethic, you
mean,' Tatiana shot back.

'You were right the first time.' Eugenie raised her
voice as her uncle moved away. 'No, you're down that
way, Uncle Nik,' the girl called, pointing in the opposite
direction from where her uncle was heading.

'No, kiddo, I think I'm sitting here.' Nik picked up one
of the place cards and held it up to show her his name.

His niece frowned, pulling a slim tablet from her
pocket. 'But I thought...'

Her mother leaned in and closed the tablet. 'It's fine,

love,' she said drily, picking up a card from the floor and, glancing at the name on it, placing it at a gap on another table.

Her brother reacted to the pointed look she sent him with an unrealistic innocent expression.

Watching the interplay, Chloe had a sinking feeling, and so she was unsurprised when the teenager smiled at her and directed her towards where Nik was holding out a chair next to his place.

Chloe's eyes brushed his and her stomach vanished completely!

The prospect of spending the entire meal next to him made her feel nauseous. *Oh, get over yourself, Chloe,* she told herself sternly. *What's the worst that can happen—you get indigestion?*

'Now, isn't this nice?' The innocence was gone and instead there was a feral gleam of challenge in his steady stare as he stood behind the chair waiting for her to take her seat. 'So cosy,' he murmured, pushing in the chair neatly behind her legs before taking his own seat.

*Cosy?* Huh. Chloe decided, nodding to the woman seated to her right, that was the last word she would use where Nik Latsis was concerned, so she didn't voice any of the half-dozen sarcastic responses that trembled on her tongue. The best way to cope with this situation was simply not to rise to the bait; instead, she would rise above it.

'Thank you,' she murmured, rather pleased with her aloof little nod, a nice combination of condescension and coldness. Yes, she decided, the high ground was *definitely* the route to take in this situation. Right but not very easy when even without looking at him she could feel the male arrogance he was radiating.

He set his elbows on the table and looked at her. 'You're dying to ask me, so go ahead.'

She squared her shoulders, and took a long swallow of the very good wine, looking at the plate that had been put in front of her; it smelt fantastic but she had virtually no appetite. 'Sorry, I don't know what you mean.'

'I'll put you out of your misery, then. You're right, Lucy and I are not a couple, just, as they say, good friends.'

'Well, that's a relief. I wouldn't have been able to sleep tonight if you hadn't explained that to me.'

Far from annoying him, her sarcastic riposte drew a broad grin. 'Ana often invites potential mates to her cosy little dinners.'

'This dinner isn't little or cosy or, as it happens, all about you.'

A smile quivered across his lips. 'Ouch!'

'You could always try dating agencies, which would be a bit more scientific than relying on your sister to set you up,' she suggested.

'I've always thought a sense of humour is overrated, especially when I'm the joke. Ana wants to see me settled down; she thinks that marriage is the magic bullet that will solve all my problems. She means well but it can get...tiresome. But you don't want to know all that; the point is... Lucy isn't my girlfriend.'

'Why are you telling me this?'

'Because I want you to say yes when I ask you to come home with me tonight.'

Having delivered this conversational dynamite in the same manner a normal person would discuss the weather, he calmly turned to the man on his right and inserted himself into the conversation concerning the most recent banking scandal.

Chloe couldn't hear what they saying, because she couldn't hear anything much beyond the static buzz inside her own head. Of course, she was going to say no to him.

She rested her hand on her thigh, running her fingers lightly across the raised damaged skin under the fine blue silk. The outline of the ugly ridges beneath her fingertips had an instant mind-clearing effect, and the doubts fluttering around in her head vanished. A man who hadn't bothered hanging around to say goodbye the morning after they'd had mind-blowing sex wasn't interested in her emotional journey; he only wanted perfect.

'I used to be a fan of your blog…is there any chance of you resurrecting it?'

Chloe snapped clear of her reverie before it reached self-pitying territory and smiled at the woman sitting across from her who'd just asked her a question. 'Well, never say never, but at the moment I can't see it happening.'

The woman looked disappointed. 'You were very successful and you had so many followers, but I suppose you've got your hands full at the moment.'

Nik had disengaged from the conversation he was involved in and took an indulgent time out to study Chloe, watching as the fine muscles along her firm jawline quivered beneath the smooth creamy skin. Her long fingers tightened around the stem of her wine glass, and he noted the absence of rings.

'So what is this blog I keep hearing about?' Nik asked curiously.

He had just announced his intention of inviting her to spend the night in his bed and now he was making small-talk! Did he compartmentalise his life as neatly as he did his conversations? she wondered, envying him the ability.

'It was a fashion blog. I started out just writing about things that caught my attention, fashion tips, current style

trends, that sort of thing, and it took off after your sister—'
she glanced towards Tatiana '—gave me a plug.'

'Was?'

She nodded and directed her gaze to the wine swirling around in her glass. The crystal caught the light of
the chandelier that hung over the table, sending little
sparks of colour through the flute. 'I've moved on to
other things.'

Dreams were not reality, they were an exaggerated,
distorted form of it, and Nik had assumed his memory
had been guilty of making some editorial cuts, smoothing out the flaws and adding a rosy tinge to the reality
of the woman who had shared her body with him. *Sharing* hardly seemed an adequate description for the lack
of barriers that had existed between them—but actually
sitting beside her now, he realised that the reality was
even better than his memory. And she'd been a virgin—
her cagey reaction had virtually confirmed his stab in
the dark—but it still didn't seem possible.

'I suppose a lot of people would get bored quickly if
they didn't have to worry about paying the rent, *Lady*
Chloe.'

His efforts to needle her into a response were rewarded
when she slung him an angry glare and drained her glass
in one gulp.

It was not the first time that someone had added the
title and her background together and come up with the
totally inaccurate conclusion that she was a lady of lei-
sure who didn't have to work for a living.

They weren't to know that, although her family had
the aristocratic family tree and the castle that came with
it, they didn't have any money, which accounted for the
holes in the roof, the ancient plumbing and the fact she
and her sister had always been expected to work for their

living. Of course, it didn't make them poor by most people's standards but the man sitting there judging her was not *most* people.

Even at this table, where conservative estimates of all the guests' wealth were eye watering, he was probably worth more than them all combined.

Her indignation fizzed hot under the surface as she fixed him with a smile of dazzling insincerity and batted her lashes like the social butterfly he seemed to think she was.

'Oh, and how I envy the *little* people with their *simple* lives... I've even heard that some people don't bathe in ass's milk or have anyone to put toothpaste on their brushes for them.'

'Did I say something to annoy you?' His glance slid from her blazing eyes to her tightened lips and his body stirred involuntarily as he remembered kissing them, tasting her... The need to do so again as soon as possible made his body do more than stir.

She shuddered out a breath and their gazes connected. Chloe was aware that she was breathing too fast as she fought to escape the message that seemed to vibrate with a palpable force in the air between them.

'You breathing annoys me!' *Too much honesty, Chloe,* she thought, aware she had lost her moral high ground the moment the childish admission left her lips, but at least she was no longer thinking about kissing him, which was good. Taking a deep breath, she glanced around to see if anyone had heard her comment. Greatly relieved when it seemed they hadn't, she directed a straight look at him. 'Look, Tatiana is a friend and I don't want to be rude to her brother.' *Or go to bed with him.*

'Or alienate a potential donor?'

Chloe realised guiltily that the sobering reminder was

necessary. She *was* in danger of forgetting that tonight was about getting the charity off the ground. Tatiana had done her bit, inviting people with deep pockets who were sympathetic to Chloe's aims, but the rest was up to her.

It was a crowded market; there were so many good causes around Chloe knew that she needed to make a positive impression on these people if she was going to make a difference.

'True, and all donations are gratefully received.'

'You already have Ana on board, so how long have you two known one another?'

'She took an interest in my fashion blog, but we'd never met. We actually met in person only a year ago, a few months after the—' She stopped abruptly, her lashes lowering in a protective sweep.

'After what?' Against his better judgement, her sudden impersonation of a clam made him curious, and, even though he knew on one level that this should be an exercise in exorcising his demons, he found he really wanted to know what made her tick.

'After I got bored with it,' she countered, deliberately not analysing her reluctance to discuss the accident with him. She applied herself to her starter, trying to simulate an interest in her food, which she couldn't even taste.

Nik, who continued to ignore his own food, propped an elbow on the table and studied her. 'So what do you do now, besides selling raffle tickets?'

'I'm working to raise the profile of the charity.'

For *working*, Nik translated, she had probably arranged a charity fashion show or a masked ball, which was fine, but hardly enough to stimulate someone of her obvious intelligence. His dark brows flattened as he recognised but struggled to explain a sense of disappointment.

It wasn't as though he had any expectations of her, and God knew she wouldn't be the only titled socialite who didn't hold down a real job. Maybe it was just that he was surrounded by strong, driven women. His mother was a partner in a law firm, who had raised brows when she had continued to work after she was married, and his sister juggled a successful career with motherhood. Ana might be in the fashion industry, but he knew that his sister would have been appalled if her daughter had thought being decorative was more important than getting an education, which made this friendship with Chloe all the more puzzling. He really couldn't see what the two women had in common.

'I don't have my wallet with me, but I do have my chequebook and I am a dutiful brother,' Nik said.

Before Chloe could react to the patronising undertone that brought a sparkle of annoyance to her eyes, across the table an elderly silver-haired Greek businessman began to laugh.

'I wouldn't be so quick to give her a blank cheque, my boy. If that young lady gets you in a headlock, she's relentless.'

Nik elevated a dark brow. 'I thought that was just a rumour.'

'She's cost me more than my wife.'

'Which one, Joseph?'

The question caused a ripple of laughter around the table.

'It's all in a good cause,' Tatiana said, patting his hand. The soft murmur of agreement that followed her words left Nik feeling excluded, as he seemed to be the only one who didn't have a clue what the old man was talking about.

'And what *cause* would that be?'

The rest of the table had returned to their own conversations and Nik's curiosity was the only thing left to
distract himself from the ache in his groin. Messing with
the seating arrangements had seemed like a good idea
at the time, but he really hadn't factored in the painful
strength of the hard throb of need, which was becoming
increasingly impossible to think past.

*Insane...* When had a woman made him feel like this?
He looked at her mouth, remembering how it had tasted,
and wondered. Last night about three a.m. she had vanished from his dreams like mist, as she always did. What
if he woke up with her in his arms for real? Would she
and the nightmares be gone for ever?

Chloe shifted in her seat before looking up from her
contemplation of her empty glass. Strands of blonde hair
fell across her cheek and she brushed them away, puzzling at her own reluctance to discuss the subject so passionate to her heart. It struck her as ironic considering
she'd spent the evening selling the cause, and in all honesty she felt she was pretty good at it.

'Helping burns victims. Originally the idea was to
raise money for specialised equipment for the NHS that
under normal circumstances they can't afford.'

It was the last thing he had expected to hear. 'And
now?'

'Oh, we'll still do all those things, but, in conjunction
with that goal, we are also aiming to set up centres where
there is access to physical therapy like physiotherapy, re-
habilitation and so forth, alongside psychotherapy and
counselling, plus the practical stuff like learning how
to apply make-up to cover scarring and job retraining.
In essence it will be a one-stop shop where people can
access what they need or just come in for a cup of coffee and a chat.'

He watched her face change as she spoke and the animation was not something that could be faked. She was truly passionate about this charity. 'That is a very ambitious scheme for someone so young.'

She lifted her chin. 'I really don't see how my age has anything to do with it, and I was always brought up to aim high.'

'So you're saying positive thinking works miracles?'

'I'm not after miracles. Everything we are aiming for is achievable and I have the facts and figures to prove it. As for positive thinking...well, that is helpful, but there comes a point when action is needed. This isn't some sort of game to me.'

'I can see that.' His admission came with some reluctance. He didn't want to admire her; he wanted to bed her. *Liking* was not a prerequisite for compatibility in the bedroom. In fact, it was a complication.

'So why this particular cause?' he asked.

'I met someone in hospital...'

'You were ill?' He visualised an image of her lying in a hospital bed and didn't dare analyse the emotion that tightened in his gut.

She dodged his interrogative stare and looked down at her fingers, watching as they tightened around the stem of the wine glass she held. She had recovered her composure by the time she responded, explaining in a quiet measured voice wiped clean of any emotion, 'I parted company with a motorbike.' The shaky laugh was less planned. 'Or so they tell me.'

The how and why remained a blank to this day. In fact the only thing she remembered that might not have been a dream was climbing on the bike calling to her sister to follow her, and then nothing until the smell of burning and sirens. If it hadn't been for her brother-in-law she wouldn't even remember that.

She wouldn't be here at all.

Some people needed their drug of choice to be happy, but she was alive and that was all the buzz she needed. The knowledge that life was so fragile had made her determined to do something with her life that would leave something tangible behind.

'I hope the driver didn't get off scot-free.' The corners of his mouth pulled down in disapproval as he imagined her slim arms around some leather-clad idiot, her lithe body pressing into him.

'I wasn't riding pillion.' It occurred to her that her pride was misplaced; after all, how well had the going-solo scenario been serving her so far?

The problem with being so independent was that when you messed up there was no one else to share the blame with.

'So you like to be in charge?'

'In charge? If by that you mean do I like to make my own decisions, then, yes, I do,' she told him calmly. 'It's never been my fantasy to be dominated by a male chauvinist.' *Just a bit too much protesting there, Chloe!*

'You're a risk taker, then?'

Holding his gaze and reacting to the challenge glittering in the ebony depths was about the most dangerous thing she had done in a long time. 'I'm not the one who made a living dodging bullets.'

He stiffened, and their eyes connected once more. The shadows in his gaze belonged to a man who had seen far too much trauma for one lifetime. A moment later his expression shuttered and the change was so abrupt that Chloe was momentarily disorientated.

'It's a phase I grew out of.'

It was the bleakness in his voice that made her realise she hadn't imagined it. For a few seconds she was back in the bar, turning without really knowing why and seeing him sitting there, the most handsome man she had ever seen or actually imagined. In the confusing mesh of emotions—attraction colliding with empathy—she'd felt the pain he was unconsciously emanating.

Dragging her thoughts back to the present, she extinguished the ache of empathy with a large dose of objectivity. *You don't need another cause,* she warned herself, *and you definitely don't need this man.*

'So was anyone else hurt in the accident?'

'Several people, including my brother-in-law, though he wasn't then…my brother-in-law, that is. Apparently there had been an oil spill earlier on a blind bend and… it just happened. There was no one to blame but me and fate.'

He tipped his chair back to look at her, though it was hard to read his expression thanks to the thickness of his long lashes. 'So you believe in fate?'

She shrugged. 'I believe you make choices and have to live with the consequences.'

'Well, you don't seem to have suffered too many long-lasting consequences.'

He really had no idea. She struggled not to touch her leg again, and instead let her eyelids lower, shading her expression with her own long, curling lashes. 'I was very lucky,' she agreed quietly.

'So what else do you believe in?' He believed in very little and he found himself almost envying her her idealism, but equally he was disturbed by the idea that it might have been some form of this idealism that had first led her to his bed, or him to hers… Had she seen him as some sort of romantic hero or had it meant nothing to her beyond a rite of passage?

He wasn't actually sure which possibility disturbed him more.

'I believe in the resilience of human spirit, I believe that you should never take anything for granted and I believe…' She gave a sudden self-conscious laugh, her eyes sliding from his. 'I believe that I'm in danger of boring you.'

It came as a shock to realise that they had reached the coffee stage.

'I'd prefer to be dead!'

The horrified exclamation by one of the female guests coincided with a lull in the conversation.

'So what is it you prefer death to, my dear?' The man to her right voiced the question on everyone's mind.

'Being a size fourteen!' She gave a theatrical shudder. 'Can you imagine?'

Chloe sat there and imagined what this woman would say if she saw the scars on her thigh. She knew full well that her reaction would not be unique.

'She's an eating disorder waiting to happen and the sad thing is she has a daughter who she'll probably pass on her neuroses to.'

Anger struck through Chloe; while she might have agreed with the sentiment Nik had privately voiced in her ear, she doubted he had ever dated a woman who carried any extra weight.

'So I suppose appearances don't matter to you,' she charged bluntly. 'You'd date someone who wasn't perfect, would you? You honestly wouldn't care if your wife gained a hundred pounds or suddenly went bald.'

His brows lifted at the heat of her accusation. 'That

sounds rather personal. Were you an ugly duckling before you became a swan? A fat child with acne...or is that a wig you're wearing...?'

She reared back as he went to touch her hair.

'You switched the place cards, didn't you? So you could sit next to me and drive me around the bend.'

'You didn't answer my question.'

'You didn't answer mine.'

He tipped his head in acknowledgment. 'I have some skills,' he admitted modestly. As he spoke he held out his hand and turned it over, extending his long brown fingers. Then with a flick of his wrist he produced one of the place cards from the sleeve of his opposite hand. 'Distraction and sleight of hand. I have other skills.'

She compressed her lips and made a point of not asking him what they were.

'Have you thought about what I said about you coming home with me tonight?'

She choked gently on her mouthful of wine before giving him a direct look. 'I assumed you were joking.' She was quite pleased with the compromise; it was a way of saying no without injuring his male ego.

Unfortunately, he didn't appear to appreciate the favour she was doing him. 'Then I'll have to think of a way of showing you that I'm not.'

Her nerve ends tingling in response to the throaty purr of his challenge, she gave a little gasp and knocked over a glass as she bolted to her feet. Aware that people were looking at her, she calmly folded her napkin and dabbed at the damp spot on the snowy cloth. 'Send me the dry-cleaning bill,' she joked.

People responded to her quip with smiles and barely looked at her as she walked around the table to where Tatiana sat.

'I promised to ring the palace to check on…'

Tatiana's sympathy was instant. 'Of course. Use my office if you want some privacy, then join us for coffee in the drawing room.'

# CHAPTER FIVE

SHE LISTENED TO her sister, who spoke at some length on the joys—*not*—of morning sickness. It wasn't until she hung up that Chloe identified the odd achey tightness in her chest as envy, but she refused to acknowledge it. Her sister deserved her happiness; it just made her aware of the things she didn't have and maybe never would.

Catching the self-pitying direction her thoughts were taking, she got to her feet, but halfway to the drawing room she chickened out and slipped into the bathroom, where she spent a great deal of time admiring the decor.

Sometimes discretion was *definitely* the better part of valour. Hoping no one had sent out a search party for her, she waited there long enough to be sure that her arrival would coincide with people leaving. Hopefully she could slip away unnoticed without any further confrontations with Nik.

She had just stepped out into the hallway when she heard Lucy's voice and ducked back into the bathroom. It was instinctive and she felt foolish the moment she locked the door. It wasn't Lucy she was hiding from, but that didn't matter; it was the fact she was hiding at all that filled her with self-disgust.

With a sigh she turned, dumped her bag on the vanity

unit and, palms flat on the marble surface, she looked at herself in the mirror.

Her face illuminated by the spotlights above looked pale and her eyes were too bright. She leaned in and touched the fine skin under her eye; the make-up helped but did not quite conceal the blueish half-moon, which was the result of a week of disturbed nights that had preceded her decision not to continue with further surgery.

The decision had felt liberating, she'd felt completely in control and yet what had it taken to throw that equilibrium into chaos? One single encounter with Nik Latsis. She made a sound of disgust in her throat and turned her back on the mirror.

She sighed. She hadn't felt in control tonight, she'd felt... She shook her head, unable...unwilling to examine her emotions as she turned, taking care not to look in the mirror, and twisted the cold tap onto full.

She stood there with her wrists under the running water, waiting for her heart rate to slow, wanting to reject outright the idea that she was attracted to Nik Latsis. The lie would have been easy, easier than admitting a man like him would never want someone less than perfect, but she couldn't.

It was a fact.

She turned off the tap, lifted her chin and looked at herself in the mirror.

'It is what it is, Chloe.'

She made her way back downstairs, where the hallway was empty but the door stood open. There was no sign of Tatiana, so she decided to call for a cab before saying goodbye to her hostess.

She had started to punch in the number when a voice at her elbow made her jump.

'Have you been hiding?' Nik asked.

'What?'

He was wearing a long tailored dark overcoat that hung open, his hair glistened wet and the same moisture glistened on his face. He had brought the smell of outdoors and rain into the room.

Chloe struggled to hide her dismay and the illicit excitement that made her stomach muscles quiver. 'You haven't gone yet.'

'Ever the gentleman, I have been escorting the ladies to their cars.' He held up a large umbrella.

Chloe clenched her fingers over her phone, ignoring the little ribbons of warm electricity making her aware of the tingling nerve endings in her skin. 'I'm just ringing for a taxi.'

He watched as she began to punch in a number, noticing that her face had a fresh scrubbed look as though she'd taken off her make-up. She still looked good, very good, but she looked more vulnerable...delicate, even. He felt an emotion swell in his chest but refused to acknowledge it as tenderness.

'You don't need a taxi.'

The harshness in his voice drew her glance upwards. 'Thanks, but no, thanks,' she said firmly, ashamed of the moments of self-pity she had indulged in.

'You're still here!' Tatiana's relieved voice rang out before Nik could respond.

Chloe was glad of the interruption but puzzled by the older woman's sense of urgency. 'I was just ringing for a taxi before I came to say goodbye, but did I forget something?' She nodded to Lucy who had appeared behind her host; the redhead was wearing a denim jacket over the slinky red dress and carrying off the contrast in considerable style.

Tatiana shook her head. 'Spiros just rang to warn anyone left not to try taking…well, just about any road, I think. The peaceful protests apparently turned out not to be so peaceful, and the police have closed down half the streets. Spiros is stuck, and he saw a car alight too. I really think it would be better if you all stay here for the night. There are reports of the disturbances spreading and even looting.'

'I'm walking home, so it's no problem,' Lucy said.

Tatiana looked alarmed.

Lucy put her hands on the older woman's shoulders. 'Relax, I'm not going to my home, I'm booked into the new boutique hotel around the corner. It's only a hundred yards, so I think I'll be safe.' She air-kissed Tatiana and thanked her, landed a kiss on Nik's cheek and waved to Chloe. 'Interesting night.'

Chloe didn't even try and translate this cryptic utterance.

'And I'm going Chloe's way so that's her problem solved,' Nik announced in a tone that brooked no argument.

Not from where she was standing!

'How do you know which way is my way? That is,' she continued, lowering the levels of antagonism in her voice, 'I wouldn't dream of bothering you.'

'Nonsense!' Tatiana sent her brother a warning glare. 'He's fine with it, aren't you, Nik?'

Chloe clenched her teeth as, with a totally unconvincing display of meekness that made him look even more like a wolf, he tipped his dark head.

'Absolutely.' Slower than Tatiana to jump back squealing when he shook the umbrella, sending a spray of cold water droplets that hit everything in the immediate area, Chloe was the only one close enough to hear his not at all meek-sounding addition. 'My way is whichever way you're going.'

She brushed her ear where the sensitive flesh still tingled from the touch of his warm breath and glared at him, while he continued to look smugly satisfied with himself.

'Well, that's sorted, then,' Tatiana said, looking relieved. 'You will text me when you get home safely?'

Chloe promised.

She gave a sigh and rubbed the tip of her nose with her finger. The truth was, there was a part of her, a clearly twisted part of her, that had...*enjoyed* their flirtation. No, that was the wrong word. It hadn't been flirtation; that was far too gentle. Combat probably better described the heart-thumping, skin-tingling adrenaline charge of their exchanges tonight.

She had felt what...? *Like a woman.* Her eyes flew wide with shock as the recognition of her too-long-suppressed sexuality crashed through her.

'Are you all right?' Nik asked.

'I'm fine!' she lied.

She read criticism in his eyes as they swept her face. 'You look like you're in pain.'

'The only pain around here...' at the last second she managed to apply the brake to her runaway tongue and lowered her eyes, muttering '...is a slight headache.'

Actually pain was pretty accurate for what she felt, as though the circulation were returning to a limb deprived of blood. It hurt and so did this—the part of her that had been in hibernation since the accident had finally woken up and it was tingling!

She wasn't ready yet; she wanted that part to go back to sleep. It was such awful bad timing! At this point an affair of any kind, let alone the sort of superficial no-strings fling Nik Latsis had in mind for them, was the last thing she needed.

She lifted her chin, defiance sparking in her eyes, as she thought, *I deserve more than that! I deserve better than Nik Latsis!*

Even if she had been in the market for a man, which she wasn't, he would not have made the shortlist. If she had needed reminding, and she didn't, how shallow he was, tonight would have driven the point home to her.

Yes, she was attracted to him, it was actually too exhausting to try and pretend otherwise, but in her defence he had more sexual charisma in a single hair follicle than most men had in their entire bodies. Although *attraction* hardly came close to describing the visceral reaction he evoked just looking at him... *Then don't look!* she told herself.

She needed to stop over-analysing everything. Nothing was going to happen between them because it couldn't. She brushed her leg with her hand, not that the numbed scar tissue registered the touch. She found herself wishing fiercely for a moment that the numbness went even deeper, that she could anaesthetise the emotions that tonight had reawoken in her.

She squared her shoulders. If he had been the Nik who had vulnerabilities, and not this insensitive, slick predator, she might have been in trouble, but he wasn't, so she was completely safe.

As safe as being circled by a tiger, she thought, injecting as much grateful insincerity into her smile as she could.

'I hope it's not too far out of your way, Nik.'

It was Tatiana who replied. 'Don't be silly, Chloe...'

'Looks like that's settled, then.' Nik walked ahead and left Chloe to walk beside his sister. When they reached the open front door she realised with a stab of shame that she didn't have a clue what the other woman had just been saying to her.

This had to stop, she told herself. Nik Latsis was the past, not a mistake because the last few months had taught her that thinking about mistakes meant you couldn't move forward. She had moved forward and she would continue to do so.

'It's stopped raining.' Nik, who had walked outside ahead of the women, lowered the umbrella he had raised and held up his hands to the sky. He grinned, twirled the umbrella and stamped in a puddle.

Fighting the urge to run out and join him, Chloe was conscious of an ache in her chest. She snatched a quick breath, knowing that the image would stay with her, but not knowing why...or at least not asking herself why.

'You're welcome to stay over if you like.'

Her friend was looking concerned as she reiterated her offer; if Tatiana had picked up on her distress, Chloe just hoped she hadn't picked up on the cause! She was tempted, she really was, but accepting the offer would mean she was afraid to be alone with Nik. And she wasn't, because nothing was going to happen between them. Chloe gathered herself and turned with a smile that felt stiff and forced, although she was unwilling to admit that even to herself.

'Thanks, but no, it would be good to get home.' She raised her voice a little to make sure that Nik could hear what she was saying and get the message. 'I'd like to sleep in my own bed.' The way her mind was working overtime she doubted there would be much sleep for her tonight.

After a pause, Tatiana nodded and kissed her cheek. 'Take care...and drive carefully, Nik,' she called after her brother, who lifted an arm and waved.

* * *

Chloe trudged on head down, Nik beside her, not touching her but close, close enough for her to be aware of the tension that stopped him dead in his tracks at the sound of distant sirens.

He stood there, head sharply angled, his lean, tense stance making her think of a wolf sensing danger, nostrils flared, scenting it in the air.

The sound retreated and he shook his head as though clearing it before glancing down at her. 'I'm parked over here.'

It took Chloe a moment to recover from the expression she had glimpsed on his face before she fell into step beside him.

'Are you all right?' she asked softly. Haunted; he had looked haunted.

He glanced down at her, the sounds of war, the explosions, the disembodied screams and the discordant staccato peal of shells still sounding in his head. 'The silences in between the shelling were the worst. Somehow they tapped into a man's primitive fears...the calm before the storm.' He stopped and the street light above them showed the shock reflected on his face...as if he'd only just realised he'd spoken his thoughts out loud.

Then it was gone, as quickly as it had appeared.

Another time his car, a low, gleaming monster, would have drawn a sarcastic remark from Chloe about macho power statements, but all she did was slide into the passenger seat when he opened the door.

She ached for his pain but she knew she couldn't let him into her life...every instinct of self-preservation told her this. The memory of that morning waking alone, when she'd waited for him, imagining the reasons for his absence—he'd stepped out for coffee, he'd gone to find a red rose—made her cringe, but even worse was when the penny had finally dropped and she had acted like someone heartbroken.

The memory she filed away as water under the bridge. Mistakes were fine—it was repeating them that was unforgivable! He was a fragment of her history and, after all, you were never supposed to forget your first lover. Well, only time would tell and she was an optimist.

'I need to stop off at the office first...there are some contracts I must sign tonight,' he said.

Any delay, any reason to prolong the time she spent in this enclosed space with him filled her with dismay, although it was mitigated with a relief that he was sounding normal again. If he was acting she was glad...she simply couldn't deal with his trauma and her own reaction to it. A vulnerable Nik was a very dangerous Nik to her peace of mind!

'At this time of night?' Her voice sounded calm but her agitation revealed itself in the smooth stroking motion of her hands as she moved them up and down over her silk-covered thighs.

'I think they'll let me in,' he said, thinking about how her legs had wrapped tight around him as he'd thrust inside her.

'Of course,' she said, feeling stupid...then something more uncomfortable than stupid when she realised his eyes were following the mechanical motion of her hands. She stopped and folded her arms defensively across her chest.

He cast a glance across her face and was distracted for a moment because she was chewing her plump lower lip and all he had to do was bend in a little closer to taste it for himself.

'Look, Nik, tonight I think I might have... If I seemed

like I wanted you to...' She swallowed and stopped; if she really hadn't wanted Nik to flirt with her, why hadn't she just told him straight out about the scars that remained after the operations, the puckered, discoloured patches of flesh on her right thigh? It would have been amusing to see how fast he retreated.

Except it wouldn't have been *amusing*.

She told herself that people's attitudes to her scars were their problem, not hers, and most of the time she believed it, but there was a world of difference between theory and fact, not to mention a world of humiliation, and she wasn't ready for that yet.

'You were saying...?' he prompted, wondering if she knew how expressive her face was. The drift of emotions across it was almost like watching a silent film.

'I think it's a very bad idea to try and relive something that happened in the past. Much better to remember it as it was.'

'So am I a happy memory or a bad one?'

'A bit of both,' she admitted, thinking that she had reached the stars with him and discovered the depths of despair. She buckled her belt, reminding herself that self-pity was for people who did not have a life and she did. She was not going to waste her time thinking about what she'd lost; she was going to celebrate what she had.

Nik watched her, the knot of frustration in his belly tightening the muscles along his jaw. He enjoyed a challenge as much as the next man but this was different... He swore under his breath as he started the engine.

'So how long have you lived in London?' he asked in an attempt at a normal conversation.

'I went to college, but I wasn't very academic...'

'You dropped out?'

'More like I was invited to leave, which was fine because I had begun to make money with the blog, which seemed so amazing at the time. I've always been lucky.'

'And accident prone,' he commented.

'People died in that accident so I was still lucky,' she retorted.

'I'm guessing you are a glass-half-full kind of person.'

'I really hope so...' She turned her head to look at the glass-fronted building he had pulled up in front of.

'I won't be long.' He leaned across and snatched the phone she was nursing on her knee.

A moment later he tossed it back to her. 'My number's in it, and if you see or hear anything, call me,' he directed sternly.

It took her a few moments to realise what he meant. Some of her antagonism faded, but she remained sceptical that his caution was warranted.

'I think Spiros might have been exaggerating the danger.' Other than the initial couple of distant sirens, which was not exactly unusual, they had encountered nothing that suggested widespread rioting.

'You might be right.' He gave a concessionary nod and slid out, closing the door behind him with a decisive click.

Chloe leaned back in her seat, relaxing enough for her shoulder blades to actually make contact with the leather, and she watched him walk away, his hands thrust deep in his pockets, up the shallow steps to the building. He paused for a moment and she heard the decisive click of the car doors locking.

'I don't believe it!'

There was no one to hear her exclamation, and her angry bang on the window went unnoticed. Then there was nobody but the uniformed security guard, who'd come out when Nik went in, who just stood there ignoring her, his eyes constantly scanning the areas to left and right.

When Nik reappeared exactly three minutes fifteen seconds later, the two men shook hands and exchanged a few words before the man walked back into the building and Nik got into the car.

Chloe stared stonily ahead as he flung some files onto the back seat. 'You locked me in.'

'I didn't want any looters stealing my car.'

She compressed her lips. 'That man ignored me—'

'That man is an ex-marine. He knew what you were doing.'

'Oh. Do you have a lot of ex-marines working for you?'

'The transition is not always kind to men who have given their lives to protect us. Dave, back there, flung himself on a landmine and saved three others in his squad, but he lost a leg below the knee.'

Their eyes connected and in his dark gaze she saw something she didn't want to acknowledge. In seconds the heat banked inside her burst into life, starting low in her pelvis and spreading out until her entire body was suffused by the same blazing fire. The instant conflagration scared her witless... It was a warning, she told herself, a warning that said if she had an ounce of self-respect she'd get the hell out of that car right now.

Panic hit her hard. 'Stop the car.' She used the anger when he ignored her to drag herself free of the last of the dangerous languor that lingered in her brain. 'I said, stop the car,' she said calmly.

He took his eyes off the road to briefly glance at her face and she could hear the irritation in his voice. 'Don't be stupid.'

The only stupid thing she had done so far was getting

into this car with him and Chloe had every intention of keeping it that way.

'You're acting as though we have unfinished business, but that's not the case. Look, I spent the night with you, end of story. It is not something I have any wish to repeat.'

'So you want to pretend it didn't happen at all.'

The suggestion, his tone, his attitude they all struck a jarring note inside her, so she counted to ten and fought to dampen the resentment she knew she had no right to be feeling.

'I'm not pretending it didn't happen; I'm admitting it shouldn't have.'

'I—'

'Get down!'

It was the tone as much as the terse instruction that made her stomach clench. 'What's wrong?'

'Just do it. There's a blanket there, cover yourself with it and duck down.' The odd instruction was delivered in a light, calm tone, but when she leaned forward and saw what he had already seen, she didn't feel very calm at all.

Ahead of them the road was filled with crowds of people. Some had banners and some carried dustbin lids, which they were banging.

He wound down the window and the suggestion of noise became a loud, discordant din.

'They sound mad.' Fear fluttered in her belly.

'They are a mob.' And it was the nature of the beast, anger and unpredictability, the pack-animal mentality, that could make the whole group do things that as individuals they would never dream of doing.

'I don't like this,' she said, once again gnawing at her plump lower lip, a nervous habit she'd never managed to break.

'I would be more concerned if you did. Duck down and pull the cover over your head.'

If he had faced this situation alone he would not have broken a sweat, not because he was brave or fearless, but because he had been in far worse situations, and as far as he could see the only thing he stood to lose was a car.

But he wasn't alone, and knowing that Chloe's safety was his responsibility changed everything. He had talked his way out of much worse situations, but with Chloe here he wasn't prepared to take even a calculated risk.

'No, I'm not hiding and leaving you exposed,' she stated, but her fists were clenched tightly.

'Why does beautiful so often go with stupid?' He sighed.

Her wrathful gaze met his in the mirror and he smiled. If she was angry, at least she wasn't afraid. 'Relax, *agape mou*, I will not let anything hurt you.'

She believed him, although it seemed that she ought to be more concerned about her mental well-being than her physical! She caught his arm and he paused, his eyes going from her fingers curled into the fabric, to her face. 'You're not going to do anything stupid, are you?'

'Could you be more specific?' he asked.

'I don't know...like fight them.'

He let out a loud throaty laugh. 'Me against fifty, sixty people? I don't much like those odds, but I'm sorry if I disappoint you in the hero stakes.'

'I promise you I never thought you were a hero.'

One corner of his mouth lifted in a lopsided grin and there was something about him...a combustible quality that made her think it would have been a brave person who bet against him, even if the odds were stacked against him.

'But I do think you're capable of doing something stupid.'

'Like they say, a good general chooses his field of battle. I am not good or a general but the concept holds true.'

'Are you going to drive on through them?' she asked nervously.

Nik had been going to reverse, but a glance in the rear-view mirror made it clear this was a now-or-never choice. The street on one side—he adjusted the mirror and silently corrected himself—on both sides of the road were full of people streaming towards the main artery road. It was hard to be accurate but he suspected that their options would close in seconds, not minutes.

'Hold on, this might be a little bumpy.'

She connected with his eyes and made a shocking discovery. 'You are enjoying this, aren't—?' She let out a shriek and closed her eyes as the car went into sudden reverse, travelling at what felt like the speed of light. It continued backwards even when it hit obstacles, objects in the road flung down by rioters.

The banner-waving maniacs followed initially, but they quickly fell away and by the time the car reached the gaggle of police cars the protestors were nowhere in sight.

'Wait here.'

She narrowed her eyes, tilted her stubborn little chin and thought, *Oh, yes that is* really *going to happen!* Who did he think he was, issuing orders to her? She opened her door and got out.

Two uniformed officers were already moving towards the car, and Nik walked towards them, looking calm and confident.

By the time she was within hearing distance, the police were complimenting Nik and shaking his hand.

'Thank you, sir. If all witnesses could be so clinically precise it would make our job a lot easier.'

'More resources,' the younger one said, 'would too.'

In response to a look he received from his colleague, he added a defensive, 'It's no secret that we're over-stretched.' Then he stopped as he saw Chloe coming towards them, his eyes widening.

Before he could speak to her, Nik moved, cutting off her approach. With a firm hand on her elbow, he turned back to the men. 'We won't get in your way, officers, and thank you. Come on, Chloe.'

She was hustled back to the car with equal ruthless efficiency. 'You didn't let me say a word to them! What did you think I was going to do?' she demanded as Nik folded his long length in beside her.

'Distract them from their job,' he replied succinctly.

'So what happens now?' she huffed.

'Now I take you home. The police have given me a route that should be clear and, before you ask, the Tube stations are closed, so don't even think of asking me to stop the car again.'

The rest of the journey was completed without incident and in total silence.

She waited until he had neatly reversed the car into a parking space clearly marked reserved outside her building before releasing her seat belt.

'I should thank you.'

'But you won't.'

'That's not what I...' A sound of irritation rattled in her throat. He drove her insane! 'All right, I *do* thank you.'

'It was my pleasure.'

He moved to open his door and she shook her head. 'No, don't get out; I'm fine.'

'I will see you to the door.'

'I'm not going to be ravished or kidnapped between here and there,' she said, nodding to the Georgian building behind them. Once it had housed one family; now it was split into twenty one-bedroom apartments, a bit down at heel, or, in estate-agent speak, ripe for improvement. Chloe had no cash to improve hers as she had poured all the money her blog had made into buying the place.

'Looking like that, I would not be so confident.'

'You mean I would be asking for it?' she countered crankily.

His exasperation increased. 'I mean that you are a very beautiful woman, this is a fact, and it is also a fact that a man who forces himself on a woman is no real man.' His nostrils flared in distaste. 'And a man who excuses the actions of such a person is no less of an inadequate loser.'

He got out and walked around to her side of the car, standing there silently as she got out.

She tilted her head to look at his shuttered face. 'I've offended you.'

He arched an eloquent brow.

'Sorry.'

He bowed slightly from the waist. 'Accepted.' A glimmer appeared in his eyes. 'Friends again?'

Chloe looked at the hand extended to her as if it were a viper. It was news to her that they ever had been friends, but he had got her home so she reached out.

He took her hand but not to shake it. Without his seeming to exert any overt pressure, she found herself colliding with his body.

His dark face lowered to hers. 'It's all about sleight of hand and distraction,' he whispered before his mouth came crashing down on hers.

The kiss was hard, hot and hungry as he plundered her mouth with ruthless efficiency. For a split second, shock held her immobile, then as his dark head began to lift something snapped inside her. Chloe felt it, even heard it, as she dragged his dark head back down to hers, parting her lips to invite a deepening of the slow, sensual exploration.

It was an invitation that he accepted, driving his tongue deep into the warm recesses of her mouth.

She was distantly conscious of the throaty, mewling little sounds but didn't make the connection between them and herself. Her hands curled into his jacket to stop herself falling as tongues of flame scorched along her nerve endings, and she felt a deep shudder ripple through the hard, lean body pressed close to her.

*'Oh, God!'*

Her shaken gasp seemed to break the spell.

The thud that Chloe heard when she fell back to earth seemed almost as real as the searing humiliation she felt as, still shaking, she looked up at him, to see that he was perfectly fine. Standing there as though nothing had happened, she thought, her indignation going supernova... then cooling slightly as she noticed the streaks of colour along his cheekbones and the fact he was breathing pretty hard.

At least he had put enough distance between them to make the basic stuff like breathing a whole lot easier. She tilted her head but it was impossible to make out his expression. Even with her eyes narrowed, his face was just a dark blur, which was probably a blessing of sorts because he no doubt looked as smug as a man who had just had his point proved could look.

She took a deep breath. 'I am not sure what that was meant to achieve.'

'Achieve?'

She ignored the interruption and didn't even register the odd strain in his voice.

'I already knew that you were a good kisser.' He was a good everything, that was the problem.

'So the problem is...?'

Arms crossed over her chest, she rubbed her upper arms with both hands. 'I enjoyed the night I spent with you, but I happen not to be quite as casual about sex as you are. That's not a criticism,' she hastened to assure him. 'I mean, as far as I'm concerned, each to his own.'

'So now you have developed a puritanical streak?'

She slung him a look of simmering dislike. 'Last time you looked...hurt...lost...' *And what's your excuse this time, Chloe?* 'I don't know, but—'

'You are saying you had pity sex with me.'

'No.'

'So are you looking for a deep and meaningful relationship?'

The sneering tone of his voice set her teeth on edge and tightened her expression into a glare, though she fought to keep the edge of antagonism from her voice. 'I'm not actually looking for any sort of a relationship just now, but when I am... I'd like to find a man who will accept me for who I am inside, and not care about the way I look.'

He gave a hard, incredulous laugh. 'Well, if that's the kind of man you're looking for, I'd start looking for a couple of nice cats instead, if I were you. What's so wrong with being beautiful? It's not exactly a curse; women spend their lives and fortunes trying to look like you and they never will. How is noticing you're beautiful an insult to you?'

She stuck out her small determined chin. 'I'm a hell

of a lot more than that, not that you're ever going to know, and, believe you me, that's your loss!' she flared, secreting the security card she'd extracted from her bag in her palm.

She widened her eyes and looked into the middle distance. 'Oh, my!'

As soon as he turned his head to see what she was staring at, Chloe ran to the door. Her security card swiped first time and she stepped into the foyer, slamming it shut a split second before he reached it.

She pressed the button on the intercom. 'It's all about sleight of hand and distraction.'

A reluctant smile fought its way to his lips. 'I thought you never hid.'

She might not know about distraction, but she understood about odds. Her father owned the leg of a racehorse and she knew the odds were good that if Nik kissed her again and she got another taste of that raw power, if she felt the impression of his erection grinding into her belly, instinct would take over and reason would fly out of the window.

And everything would be hot and marvellous until he got an up-close-and-personal look at the part of her that once had been perfect and now wasn't. Did she want to carry the memory of his look of disgust or embarrassment as he pulled away from her? That was a no brainer.

'I'm not hiding from you. I'm walking away. There's a difference.' The moment she turned away from him the tears she had been holding back began to fall, and, running up the stairs, she swiped at them irritably.

Just sex was really not worth it!

# CHAPTER SIX

IT WAS NOON when Chloe got back to her flat, but the first thing she did was strip off, push her clothes in the linen basket and step in the shower. The act of washing was purely symbolic; she knew the scent of hospital was in her mind, because the only thing the doctor's consulting room on the top floor of the rather beautiful Georgian building it occupied had smelt of was his expensive aftershave.

Hair still damp, she tightened the belt of her robe around her waist and flung herself down on the sofa, keying in her sister's number on her phone...but it went straight to voicemail.

With a sigh she dropped the phone in her robe pocket and padded barefoot over to the kitchen. Of course, if her sister had known about the hospital appointment she would have been waiting for the call—no, she would have come with her—but she didn't know. Chloe deliberately hadn't told anyone about it, *especially* her family.

They had been through enough during the long months after the accident—not that her choice not to tell them was entirely selfless. She knew that they, or at least her parents, would struggle to understand her decision not to have further cosmetic surgery. Down the line who knew how she'd feel about it? While it certainly was an option, right now she'd had enough of hospitals and she felt that to go through all that again was unbearable, especially as there were no guarantees regarding exactly how much improvement there would be, as the doctor would not give any promises.

She had taken a sip of her scalding coffee when her phone rang, and she lifted it to her ear and said hello.

It was not her sister who replied and, stifling a surge of disappointment, she said, 'Can you just hold on a second?' and reached out to shut the door of the fridge, which was buzzing to remind her she'd not closed it. 'Hi, Tatiana.'

'S… Sorry, is this a bad time?'

Chloe's reaction was immediate; elbows on the counter, she leaned forward, concern furrowing her brow. 'No, it's fine…is anything wrong?' When they had spoken earlier today, Tatiana had sounded relaxed and happy, issuing an invitation that Chloe had refused, which had been to join her on the family estate on the Greek island of Spetses. But now, only a few hours later, she was obviously close to tears.

'I told you, didn't I, that I agreed to Eugenie spending the first week of the holiday with her friend Pippa in Hampshire…?'

'Yes…has something gone wrong?' Chloe asked.

Tatiana gave an unamused laugh. 'You could say that. Pippa's parents in their wisdom decided that two fifteen-year-old girls were mature enough to be left alone in the house while they went away for the night.'

'Oh, dear!'

'Oh, yes, definitely *oh, dear*. The girls decided to have an impromptu party with supposedly just a few friends but, to cut a long story short, it was gatecrashed by lots of other kids, the place was wrecked and the neighbours called the police! Eugenie has been cautioned by the police and she is waiting at the local police station to be picked up. Pippa's parents have decided she is a bad influence—can you believe it? The problem is, my grandmother has a really high temperature, so I can't leave her, and my brother's not picking up his phone and no one seems to know where he is.'

'What can I do?'

A sob of relief echoed down the line. 'Could you pick her up for me and take her to the airport?'

'Of course.'

'The Gulfstream jet was in Frankfurt; I have no idea what my parents are doing there. Anyhow, I made some excuse up to say I needed the plane, but I really don't want them to know about this. It should be there by the time you arrive.'

'Don't worry, I'll drop her off safely.'

'Drop her off? Oh, no, Chloe, I need you to travel with her to Spetses, and sit on her if necessary! I'm not risking her pulling another stunt.'

It was only the rising hysteria in her friend's voice that stopped Chloe pointing out that there seemed little possibility of her daughter coming to any harm on a private flight to a Greek island. 'Fine, I'll sit on her.'

'I knew I could rely on you. Thank you so much, Chloe. I'll never be able to repay you.'

Actually, Chloe realised as she picked up her car keys, it was Tatiana who was doing her a favour. Left to her own devices she'd have spent the evening brooding over her decision and planning how she broke the news to her parents. Instead, she had plenty to distract her.

A cloudburst proved to be one of the distractions she hadn't figured on.

Chloe was drenched to the skin as she sat in the police

station studying a poster on the wall that proclaimed in large letters *Don't be a victim,* a sentiment she agreed with wholeheartedly, when Eugenie appeared walking alongside a fresh-faced policewoman who barely seemed older than the teen.

The girl's face dropped when she saw Chloe.

'I thought Uncle Nik was coming to get me.'

'Your mum couldn't contact him.' Chloe struggled not to sound judgemental about that as her imagination kicked in, supplying a slide show of selfish reasons for Nik being off the grid, all revolving around beautiful women and bed.

*Well, you declined his offer to spend the night with him,* Chloe reminded herself. *Did you expect him to go back home and weep into his beer, or did you expect him to pursue you?*

He clearly hadn't done either, which reinforced the obvious: it had been an opportunist offer, made in the heat of the moment, and when she'd refused he had chalked it up to experience and moved on.

A circumstance she told herself she was relieved about.

'Uncle Nik would understand...*he* wouldn't lecture me,' the girl said, her defiant expression suggesting that Chloe couldn't even begin to do so.

In contrast to the girl's dramatic pronouncement Chloe kept her voice light and friendly. 'I'm not here to lecture you,' she returned, thinking, *Thank God, it's not my job.* 'Just get you to your mum.'

The girl pouted and tossed her head. 'Well, you took your time.'

Chloe smiled and counted to ten. 'Yes, I thought I'd take the scenic route as it's such a lovely day for a drive.' She gestured to the window, where the rain was falling from a leaden summer sky. 'And obviously I had nothing better to do.' Without waiting for the girl's response, she turned to the policewoman. 'Thank you very much for looking after her.' She glanced at Eugenie. 'Ready...?'

The girl nodded. Minus the truculent attitude, she looked so miserable and very young standing there shifting her weight from one spiky heel to the other that it was all Chloe could do not to hug her.

Instead she slipped off her jacket and draped it over the girl's bare shoulders. 'It's a bit chilly out there.'

Eugenie turned her head to look up at Chloe. 'Is she really mad? Mum, I mean?' she muttered.

'I'm afraid I'm just the chauffeur.' Chloe hesitated, choosing her words with care. 'I've zero experience of being a parent, but I have been a daughter and when my parents were angry with me it was usually because they were worried about me.'

'There was no reason for her to be worried.'

'If you say so.'

'You don't believe me, do you?'

'I'm parked just over there.'

'Uncle Nik would believe me—he'd understand.'

*Well, bully for Uncle Nik,* Chloe thought, keeping her lips sealed over her resentment. Uncle Nik, who would no doubt have beautiful babies, and was, as far as she knew, somewhere right now trying to make one.

She frowned, rubbing her upper arms through the silk of her already drenched blouse, and pushed the accompanying image away. Wherever he was too busy to pick up his phone, it was bound to be some place nice and warm while she was drenched to the skin and walking on eggshells with a teenager who made her feel about ninety!

Just as she was on the point of deciding that parenthood was clearly a mug's game, her sulky charge stopped. Impatient, Chloe turned back.

'Thank you for coming for me,' Eugenie said in a small quivery voice.

'You are very welcome.'

Chloe fished her keys from her pocket and opened the passenger door of her own utilitarian hatchback. 'Sorry you're slumming it today.'

'*That* is your car?' The girl's astonishment was almost comical, as was her horror. Chloe strongly suspected that the idea of being seen in anything so uncool worried her more than the idea of parental ire or a jail cell.

'So what does it do, thirty with the wind behind it?'

'If we're lucky.' *Speed* had not been a priority when she had first got behind the wheel of a car after the accident, but safety had. Not that she expected the girl, or anyone else for that matter, to understand that this car represented a personal triumph for Chloe.

She could have rationalised it and it would have been easier than admitting her fears. Far easier to pretend that she was doing her eco bit for the planet by using public transport, asking how convenient actually was it to have a car in the City?

Instead she had admitted she had a problem, and her family had been proud when she had conquered her fears, but the truth was her honesty had certain limitations. She'd never told them that her hands still got clammy when she slid into the driver's seat and her heart rate took a few minutes before it settled into a normal rhythm.

Time, she hoped, would eventually finish the healing process.

'I thought you were meant to be royal or something...'

'Or something,' Chloe admitted with a laugh. 'You can always duck down if you see anyone you know—'

The sound of a car that was neither safe nor slow made them both turn as a limousine complete with blacked-out windows drew up behind them.

The girl's pale face lit up. 'It's Uncle Nik.'

Chloe already knew that. As he got out of the car her minor palpitations suddenly became critical.

'He'll understand.' The relief in the girl's face faded away to uncertainty as she realised what Chloe already had. The man striding towards them was furious.

His face set in hard lines, his dark brows drawn into a straight line above his hawkish nose, he stopped a couple of feet away from them. He was breathing hard and looked like a well-dressed version of a dark avenging angel as the wind caught the hem of his long coat, making it billow out behind him.

'What the hell did you think you were doing?'

As the teenager shrank into her side Chloe wondered if Nik knew he had gone from hero to villain in just one short sentence.

Nik's narrowed eyes followed the protective hand Chloe slid around the girl's shoulders, and his jaw tensed as he flashed her an arctic glare.

'Thank you for your...*help*.' The word emerged reluctantly through his clenched lips. 'I'm assuming that Tatiana contacted you?'

Her chin lifted in challenge. He had managed to make the statement sound like an accusation. *No, I just happened to be passing.*

It took an effort but she managed to keep her lip buttoned on the snarky retort that hovered on the tip of her tongue, and she dipped her head in acknowledgment, reflecting that surely *one* of them had to act like an adult in front of Eugenie.

'Well, I'm here now.'

As if that could have slipped anyone's notice! So this was Nik in business mode; impressed hardly covered her reaction. His designer-cut business suit didn't disguise the hardness of the body it covered, but it did emphasise the effortless power he exuded.

Nik dragged his eyes away from the outline of the lacy bra covering Chloe's breasts, clearly outlined beneath the drenched silk, just in time to see her roll her eyes at him. He wondered why, of all the people she could have turned to for help, his sister had chosen this woman, who was nobody's idea of a responsible adult. Hell, she didn't even have the basic sense to leave the house with a coat in a storm!

'Get in the car,' he ordered his niece.

'I'm not going anywhere with you!' was the response.

If his scowl was any indicator, he only saw the surly expression on Eugenie's face, and not the fact that her defiance only went about a cell deep despite the dramatic pronouncements. Clearly it wasn't his incredible insight into female behaviour that got him the girls, Chloe thought sourly.

'I hate you!'

Chloe sighed. It was a long shot, but she felt obliged to at least make an attempt to smooth things over.

'Look, clearly you're both feeling pretty intense…'

Two pairs of antagonistic eyes zoomed in on her face.

She cleared her throat and attempted a smile. As far as feelings went, her own were pretty much all over the place and had been from the moment she'd identified the person getting out of the car and her heart had started fibrillating madly. It had not even begun to calm down when he'd stalked towards them looking deliciously sexy, hard and… She gave her head a tiny shake. This wasn't about her, or her hormones; it was about Eugenie and Tatiana.

'Maybe now...' she continued, channelling sweet reason and calm while wondering if it was all right secretly wanting to do the wrong thing just so long as you actually resisted the weakness.

'Now what?' he bit out.

She dragged away her eyes, which were showing a disastrous tendency to drift up and down his long, lean, loose-limbed frame without her permission, and cleared her throat. What she needed right now was cool thinking, logic and maybe a bit of inspiration. What she didn't need or, for that matter, want was this animal attraction, insane sexual chemistry or a vivid imagination supplying her with memories of how he'd looked naked.

'Now is not the right time to—'

The teen shrugged off the arm across her shoulders and, with hands on her hips, took a defiant step towards her uncle. 'It wasn't my fault.'

Chloe sighed and wondered why she had even bothered to try. If she had any sense, which she did, she would get in her car, drive off and let these two slug it out, but then she reminded herself that Tatiana was her friend, and she had promised her she'd look after Eugenie.

Nik felt his grip on his temper slipping, but he breathed through the moment.

It had not been a good morning. He'd had a breakfast meeting with a guy the normally reliable firm of headhunters had sent, and in the space of thirty minutes the candidate had broken every unwritten rule in the book: drunk too much, confided personal problems, bad-mouthed colleagues and talked politics. Then Nik had returned to the office and found all the messages on his machine his stand-in secretary had not seen fit to respond to.

But compared to his present situation, faced with a

niece who appeared to loathe him while challenging his authority, and the woman who hadn't been out of his head for more than three consecutive seconds ever since they'd parted company nearly forty-eight hours ago, he was extremely frustrated and close to snapping point!

He'd spent the last two days considering the best way to seduce Chloe Summerville. Seduction had never had much to do with the kind of recreational sex he enjoyed; usually it wasn't about anything but slaking a hunger and for a short space of time blocking out everything else. Mutual attraction was certainly involved, but comparing it with what had sparked into life between himself and Chloe would have been like comparing a light shower with a monsoon!

And the attraction between them was mutual, he knew that without question, which made her rejection of him all the more teeth-grindingly frustrating.

He didn't make the mistake of reading anything deep and meaningful into their attraction; it was more to do with the timing and circumstances of their first meeting than anything else. Those circumstances had just intensified the chemistry that existed between them, that was all—a chemistry that would inevitably fade.

If when it did, so did his nightmares, that was only an added bonus. Getting her into bed was definitely going to happen; it was just a matter of when. His instincts could not be that far out, surely?

'Get in the car,' he repeated to his niece, digging into reserves of tolerance that had already been seriously depleted.

Chloe took a deep breath and came to a decision. Stepping forward, she put herself between the angry male and his niece. 'Actually, I promised Tatiana that I would deliver her personally, so, Eugenie, get in my car.' The slam of the car door told her that the girl had obeyed. Chloe felt a stab of relief; she would have looked pretty silly if Eugenie had ignored her.

Nik growled. He wasn't used to having his decisions challenged or his instructions ignored and suddenly the emotions that ran rampant through him had nothing to do with their natural chemistry and everything to do with the fact that Chloe was a pain in his backside! He made to move past her but Chloe mirrored his move.

She held up her hands, her expression determined.

'You think my niece needs protection from me?' he demanded incredulously, his voice pitched to a low, private rumble.

*Not half as much as I do,* Chloe thought, despising the part of her that couldn't help but notice how incredibly good he looked clean-shaven. 'Don't be absurd!' she snapped, fighting the urge to follow his lead and respond in kind. Instead she modified her tone. 'Of course I don't! It's just that in a situation like this—'

'And how many times have you been in a situation like this, *Lady* Chloe?'

'You might be surprised,' she retorted, but as the antagonistic glitter faded from his eyes she admitted, 'Fair enough, I've never been arrested, but I think you're the last person in the world to be throwing my life of imagined privilege in my face.'

'You're encouraging Eugenie to think this is a joke.'

She flung him a pitying look; for an intelligent man he was being pretty dense. 'She doesn't think it's a joke. She was scared stiff. I just think you're making a big thing out of this when—'

'My niece has been arrested. I call that a big thing!'

'She was only cautioned, and according to the sergeant I spoke to—'

A hiss of impatience left his clamped lips and she changed tactics.

'Look, Tatiana wants to keep this low-key, so you could force Eugenie to travel with you, but what would be the point? I mean, do you even know what you're letting yourself in for? Teenage girls tend to have a taste for melodrama and, I can assure you, she'd make the journey hell for you.'

'Is there a problem here?'

Chloe turned to see the policewoman from earlier standing looking at them. Well, actually she was looking at Nik and her mouth was ajar.

Chloe cleared her throat and gave the girl time to recover, as she had some sympathy for her dilemma.

'You know what it's like—you wait for a bus and two come along at once. This is Eugenie's uncle and we were just discussing it.' She turned to Nik. 'So is it OK if Eugenie comes with me?'

He didn't miss a beat. 'Absolutely and we can catch up on the way. Fred, my driver, can follow us.'

Her air of complacence vanished in an eye blink. 'You want me to give you a lift to the airport?' she squeaked, forgetting to avoid his eyes. They were shining with malicious amusement as if he knew perfectly well that the very thought of being confined inside her car with him for an hour was already making her break out in a cold sweat.

She closed her eyes and breathed out through her nose as she subdued her panic; he'd called her bluff and now she'd have to live with it. An hour was only sixty minutes, she reminded herself, yet somehow the maths wasn't particularly soothing so she decided not to work out the seconds as she watched him speak to the driver of the car.

* * *

Maybe it was wishful thinking but lately she liked to think that she was not quite as tense behind the wheel, but either way this journey was going to put her back months.

Nik was not a relaxed passenger; she could feel the tension rolling off him. Maybe he didn't like women drivers...or perhaps it was just her... He certainly couldn't be comfortable as he had to draw his long legs right up in order to squeeze himself into the space.

Served him right, she decided uncharitably as she stared doggedly ahead, ignoring him and the subtle spicy notes in the male fragrance he used.

The expression on her face when Nik had invited himself had seemed worth it at the time...but the decision had come back to bite him. The physical discomforts aside, and there were several—he had intermittent cramp in his left leg, and was losing the feeling in his foot, and the torture didn't look like being over any time soon, if ever—she drove at a maddeningly slow speed that he found at odds with her personality.

He suspected that if he mentioned it she'd go even slower just to annoy him, but when a caravan overtook them he lost the battle with exasperation. 'You drive like an old woman.'

'Sexism and ageism in one sentence...wow, impressive.'

'You haven't even got out of second gear yet.'

'Enjoy the scenery. Is he going to follow me the entire way?' She glared into the rear-view mirror that reflected the limo that was following close behind.

'That's the idea.'

'Is your driver ex-army too?'

The question startled a surprised look from him. 'What makes you say that?'

She shrugged. 'He has that look, you know, tough, hard…the catch-a-bullet-in-his-teeth type.'

Nik grinned, thinking Fred might quite like the description. 'He's a veteran.'

'You do employ a lot of ex-servicemen.'

'I'm not being charitable…'

He said it as if being considered charitable was an insult.

'I simply employ people I can rely on.'

And where he'd lived and worked, she supposed, you had to trust and rely on the people around you. 'Do you miss it…?' She bit her lip. 'Sorry, I didn't mean to remind you of…anything…'

'So Ana has been talking.'

'She mentioned what you used to do and—'

'Relax, you haven't reminded me. Losing a friend is not something you ever forget.' *Or forgive,* he thought as once again the familiar sense of guilt settled its suffocating weight over him.

She glanced in the rear-view mirror again. Eugenie had her eyes closed, and even over the engine the muffled bass boom coming from the music she was playing through her earphones was audible. 'Of course not… sorry.' She winced—the response to what he'd said seemed painfully inadequate and she pressed a hand briefly to the base of her throat where a blue-veined pulse was pounding in the hollow.

The action drew his eyes to the vulnerable spot, and the arrow-piercing thrust of raw desire caught him off guard and fed into the resentful anger he was feeling. 'If Ana has recruited you to her cause, please don't bother—'

'What cause?' She felt the suspicious brush of his dark hostile eyes over her bewildered face.

'It doesn't matter,' he said after a moment. 'My sister

is overprotective and a great believer in *talking* about everything.'

Comprehension dawned. 'Oh, she wants you to talk through your...experiences with...someone.' And for a proud man, a man used to being in control all the time, that would be anathema. She wished Tatiana good luck with that endeavour, but she didn't envy her the task of persuading her macho brother it was not a sign of weakness to talk about his feelings.

Nik's lips twisted into a cynical smile. 'How delicately put,' he mocked. 'But I don't want to forget.'

'Therapy isn't about forgetting. It's about living with the memories.'

'What would you know about it?' he jeered.

'We plan to use the services of therapists in our centre; it's an intrinsic part of the recovery process.'

'An *intrinsic* part of *my* recovery process is a glass of whisky and a night of f—'

'*Nik!*' Pretty sure what he'd been going to say and equally sure he wouldn't want to risk his niece hearing him say it, she jerked her head towards the back of the car, her eyes wide in warning.

Dark strips of colour stood out darkly against the uniform gold tones of his olive skin, emphasising the slashing angle of his high cheekbones.

In the back Eugenie began humming off-key to her music, her eyes still closed. The sound broke the awkward silence that had settled in the front of the car. 'She'll probably be deaf before she's twenty. I don't know why Ana allows her to use those things,' Nik muttered.

'Maybe you won't sound quite so disapproving when you're the parent of a teenager.' Her smile faded. The idea of Nik with children of any age was quite a depressing thought.

'Ana's a great parent,' he agreed.

Chloe was surprised to hear an unusual tone of humility in his voice, and she was even more surprised when he added, 'So is Ian.'

'I've never met him.'

'He's a nice guy, and they made a great couple. If they couldn't make it work I really don't know why anyone tries.'

'Love, maybe?'

His laugh was hard and cynical...leaving little doubt in her mind about his opinion of love.

For some reason the sound brought back a memory of another laugh, soft instead of harsh, a laugh she'd heard when her tongue had been moving across the hard pebble of his nipple, his fingers tangled in her hair, his body hot as he'd collapsed onto the bed, pulling her on top of him.

Then a minute, an hour, a lifetime later—time had stopped having much meaning—that laugh had come again as he'd rolled her onto her back, pinned her hands above her head with one hand and slid the other between her legs...

'You should be careful—you almost hit forty miles an hour then.'

His voice jolted her free of the images playing in her head and she drew her bottom lip over her upper one to blot the beads of moisture there. She felt the heat that suffused her body travel up her neck, threatening her with the mother of all blushes, so she dealt with it by choosing to pretend it was happening to someone else and it was this anonymous person who was feeling the shameful ache between her legs, not her.

'I'm trying to concentrate,' she snapped, glancing guiltily in the rear-view mirror, relieved when she saw that Eugenie was busy texting on her phone.

He looked at her fingers, which were locked, knuckles bone white, on the wheel. 'Do have you points on your licence or something?'

'Or something,' she said in a flat little voice.

He glanced in the mirror. 'She's texting again.'

'You don't know many teenagers, do you?'

'It's a day for new experiences, it seems. Is there a reason you drive this old thing?'

'Reliability.' A very underrated commodity.

'I have a reliable lawnmower but I don't go to work on it.'

'You could always get out and thumb a lift with your friend Fred.'

'That's a difficult choice. He has terrible taste in country and western music…anything involving heartbreak and tragic lives and he's happy. But if I stay with you, I might never walk again.' He grunted as he attempted to stretch out one leg in the confined space, while beside him she released her death grip on the steering wheel long enough to push a strand of hair behind her ear. Though her hair was almost dry now, the scent of her shampoo still permeated the enclosed space.

Seeing the action out of the corner of her eye, Chloe permitted herself a smirk, which she suddenly doused, feeling ashamed. Maybe she should have allowed him to take Eugenie; after all, he was her uncle.

Had she done the right thing?

The obvious thing would have been to check with Tatiana, but the thought vanished as a sharp pain made her wince and she moved her head to try and ease it. Reluctant to take her eyes off the road, especially as they had just passed a road sign that announced they were approaching a series of tight bends, she twisted her head sharply in the hope that the action would free the earring that had got tangled in her hair, but instead it just tugged harder, bringing tears to her eyes.

'Let me help...'

'I'm fine!' she snapped, unable to keep the note of panic from her voice, but then his long fingers brushed her neck and she flinched, desire clenching like a fist low in her belly.

It was crazy, she knew that, but recognising this fact did not lessen the physical impact, although she didn't have to embrace it!

'These things are lethal,' he said, lifting the weight of her hair to lessen the tug of the earring on her earlobe.

One element of her discomfort eased, Chloe stared straight ahead. Having her earlobe torn or her hair wrenched from her scalp would have been a hell of a lot more comfortable than feeling the warm waft of his breath on her cheek.

'They're one-offs, hand forged, the silversmith is a friend...' She spoke quickly, trying to distract herself.

She remembered reading somewhere that the ear had a lot of nerve endings, and all of hers were definitely screaming right now.

His brows drew together in a dark line of disapproval. 'Your earlobe is bleeding; you must have one hell of a high pain tolerance.'

An image floated into her head of her in hospital, re-peatedly pressing the pain-relief button that for weeks had never left her hand. 'Not really.' Actually, not at all, she corrected silently, thinking of the lovely float-ing feeling after she'd pressed that button. The pain had still been there in the background, but she had been able to float above it.

She felt rather than saw him looking at her.

'I fainted when I had them pierced, although that might have been the…ouch, be careful!'

'Sorry. Hold on, I've almost finished…'

*Almost* was not soon enough. It seemed to take for ever for him to unwind the silver spiral. Her relief was so intense when he gave a grunt of triumph and leaned back in his seat that she would have punched the air in triumph had she not had such a tight hold of the steering wheel. Instead, she contented herself with heaving a huge sigh.

'Cool!' Eugenie, her earphones now dangling around her neck, leaned forward and snatched the silver spiral that dangled in her uncle's fingers. 'Where did you get them from? I'd love a pair.'

'A friend of mine makes them.'

The girl moved forward asking eagerly, 'Boyfriend?'

Aware that beside her Nik was now sitting with his head bent, fingers pressed to the bridge of his nose, she shook her head. 'Her name is Layla.' She slid Nik a sideways glance and lost the fight against her concern. 'Do you have a headache? There should be some painkillers in the glove box and a bottle of water—'

'I'm fine.' He let his hand fall from his face and exhaled slowly. The headaches hit without warning, but he never took medication. Perhaps he deserved the pain, not that it ever left him feeling cleansed of his sins.

'Uncle Nik is never ill. He's bulletproof *literally*,' she enthused with awe. 'He never got a scratch when he was working in war zones,' she chattered on, lifting the earring to her own ear and craning her neck to admire the effect in the rear-view mirror. 'Mum says the only thing he's got is survivor's guilt…' She stopped abruptly as her uncle caught her eye. 'Well she might have said something like that but I don't quite recall.'

Chloe couldn't see Nik's face but she could feel the raw tension vibrating off him.

In the back seat Chloe gave a sigh. 'How much longer? It's not mine,' she added when the audible sound of a vibrating phone suddenly echoed through the car.

Nik swore. His phone had fallen in the gap between the seats and, eyes still closed, he reached out a long arm for it.

Chloe gave a grunt as an elbow landed in her ribs.

'Sorry,' he muttered and, delving further, he gave a grunt of triumph as he managed to get his fingers around it.

'Your mother,' he said to Eugenie after reading the text message, before switching his attention to Chloe. 'Telling me not to bother, not to worry, that she arranged for someone else to pick you up... I contacted her when I started out but she must have sent this straight away. Looks like you're calling the shots here.'

Embarrassed, Chloe shook her head. 'You're Eugenie's uncle.'

'My sister must really trust you, but it might take me a while to work my way back into her good graces.'

'She'll understand.'

He huffed out a laugh. 'Why should she?'

'It's what family do. Where were you anyway? Not that I have any right to ask, I know...'

'My secretary has the flu and her stand-in hadn't charged my phone.' Louise always did it for him. 'And when I said I didn't want to be disturbed I made the mistake of assuming she would know that didn't include family emergencies. She let all Ana's calls go to the messaging service and when I tried to ring her back there was no signal. Then when I asked her why she hadn't put the calls through she just burst into tears.'

'Poor woman, she was probably scared of you.'

He gave a snort of disbelief. 'Then she'll be much happier working elsewhere.'

Chloe was shocked. 'You didn't sack her!'

'My father would have, whereas I'm a much more tolerant employer and, employment laws being what they are, I just shipped her back to the department she came from.'

'You're afraid to let anyone see you have a heart,' she charged and, expecting to see him discomfited by her discovery, she turned her head to look at him, but found a very different expression on his face.

She looked away quickly, but not before the need she had seen shining in his eyes had awoken the same feeling in her belly.

He shot a quick furtive glance in the back before announcing very quietly, 'I have a heart and I am very anxious to prove it to you.'

'It's not your heart you're offering me.'

'All parts of my anatomy are on offer.'

She shivered and stared ahead. 'I'm not discussing this with you now.'

'Later, then.'

A hissing sound of frustration escaped her clenched teeth.

'Chloe...'

Chloe started guiltily at the sound of the curious voice from the back seat. 'Do you live in a castle?'

'My sister does, but where my mum and dad live is more properly termed a fortified home.'

'Normal people do not live in castles.'

'Normal people do not have a rota for the shower because there's never enough hot water to go around! Trust me, we are not at all glamorous—in fact, we're just a little bit last century. I was at college before I ordered my first takeaway pizza.'

'God!' Eugenie breathed.

'Take the next exit,' Nik said suddenly as they approached the roundabout. 'You just went past it,' he said with an air of resignation.

'Roundabouts are made for going around.' On this note of logic she did so for the third time.

# CHAPTER SEVEN

THEIR PROGRESS THROUGH the private airport was swift. Once they were on the plane one of the male attendants drew Nik apart as Chloe and Eugenie were seated.

Their conversation in rapid Greek lasted a few moments.

'I'm travelling up front,' he said to Chloe as he moved past her.

'Can I come too?' Eugenie cried in the act of unclipping her belt.

'You're grounded, or I'm assuming you will be, so no…behaving badly doesn't get rewarded, kiddo.' He flicked her nose affectionately with his finger and walked on, vanishing through the cockpit door.

'I'm going to get my pilot's licence as soon as I'm old enough. Uncle Nik got his when he was seventeen.'

Did that mean he was flying the plane now? Chloe wondered, tensing a little as the plane started taxiing; she was fine with flying but the take-off and landing always tied her stomach in knots.

Once they were in the air, Chloe accepted the offer of tea but refused anything to eat. Eugenie, who seemed to have recovered from her brush with the law, tucked into some hot beef sandwiches.

She finished and sighed in pleasure. Chloe pointed

to her chin and the teen wiped away the spot of relish there.

'So how long does it take to get to Spetses airport?'

The girl looked surprised by the question. 'Oh, there isn't an airport on the island. We land at the small private airport just on the mainland opposite and then we'll fly over on the helicopter.'

Questioning her decision not to simply hand Eugenie over to her uncle when she'd had the chance, Chloe took a sip of her tea. The return flight might not be as simple to organise as she had imagined.

On the helicopter trip over from the mainland Chloe sat next to Eugenie, who went into tour-guide mode the minute they took off. By the time they landed Chloe felt pretty well informed about the island of Spetses and its aristocratic heritage; she could have written a paper about the colourful mansions, the history of blockade running, its significance in the Napoleonic wars, and its long association with the master sailors.

While Chloe was being educated, Nik sat next to the pilot in the cockpit. The two men obviously knew one another pretty well and, with his sleeves rolled up and his dark hair tousled, Nik looked relaxed and very different from the man she remembered from that night in the bar.

Or for that matter from any time since.

It would be very easy, she mused, to let her defences down with this Nik. Just as well she was only here to chaperone Eugenie.

She turned her head at the sound of a phone ringing, struggling to make itself heard against the noise of the helicopter.

'It's Mum, for you,' Eugenie said, holding her own phone out for Chloe.

Chloe pressed the phone close against her ear, raising her voice above the background noise. 'Hello.'

'How can I ever thank you, Chloe?'

'No thanks required. I'm glad I could help.'

'How is she?'

'Fine.' She gave the worried-looking teenager a thumbs-up signal. 'I know a great deal about Spetses now. Did you know that Spetsiots were heroes of the War of Independence?' Chloe was pleased to hear the older woman laugh, then listened to her friend launch into another fulsome apology for imposing on her. 'Eugenie was no problem,' she said honestly, adding when Tatiana made sceptical noises, 'It was good practice for when I have my own children...' She lifted the phone away and waited for the static crackle to subside before shouting, 'I said it was good practice for when I have my own children!'

It was only when she realised the signal had cut out and she lowered the phone that she realised Nik was standing right beside her, so there was zero chance he'd not heard every word she'd said. But if she'd had any doubts his first comment dispelled them.

'Thinking of starting any time soon?'

Working on the assumption that if she ignored her blush he might not notice, she managed a small laugh. 'My body clock is not ticking too loudly just yet.'

'Just wanted to say, another five minutes and we'll be landing.' He turned away and moved back to the cockpit.

Once he'd gone, Chloe closed her eyes and pushed her fist against her mouth to stifle her loud groan. The other hand was pressed to her chest, where her heart was performing all sorts of life-threatening gymnastics.

It was ridiculous...bewildering and humiliating. Why did she react this way to him? What was it about him that seemed to tap into something inside her...a *need*...

a *hunger*...? An image of the answering hunger she had glimpsed in his eyes flashed into her head and her heart gave a heavy traitorous thud then started cantering crazily again.

She was complaining a hell of a lot, Chloe reflected, but if she really didn't want Nik chasing her, throwing temptation in her way, why hadn't she done something about it?

She could.

And she knew it. There was a fail-safe way, a one-hundred-per-cent-guaranteed method to make him back off at her disposal... It wasn't as if she'd even have to show him; just using the words would have the desired effect. She could casually throw into the conversation that she had some ugly scars and always would have.

In Nik's head she was perfect. She inhaled and lifted her chin, a little smile playing across her mouth. She had been perfect and she had taken it for granted. Strange how you didn't appreciate something until it was gone.

The smile vanished and along with it the enduring sadness; she'd been lucky and she knew it. She no longer wallowed in self-pity or asked herself why it had to happen to her.

She contented herself with imagining that one day there would be a man in her life; of course, he might not make her think of passionate, all-consuming sex the moment she saw him but there were other, more important things in a relationship...deeper things that lasted the test of time.

It would be nice to have both, but she was a realist and she knew few people were that lucky.

They had disembarked the helicopter when Nik joined them, his tall, broad-shouldered figure drawing glances from the handful of fellow travellers that hovered nearby. Watching his approach through the shield of her lashes, Chloe had to admit it was not surprising he drew every eye; he might be the most irritating man on the planet with an ego to match, but he was also the most supremely elegant and by far the sexiest.

'If you don't mind I'll hang around for a bit and hand Eugenie over to her mum personally,' she said.

There was a slight time delay before he responded and the enigmatic smile that briefly tugged at the corners of his mouth troubled her, but as she'd been geared up for an argument his non-reaction was a bit of an anticlimax.

'The car should be waiting; it's this way.' His gesture invited Chloe to step ahead of him.

The waiting car was another long, shiny monster, and as they approached the driver jumped out, a Greek version of Fred.

Nik called out to him in Greek, the man called something back in response and walked around to the passenger door, but before he had a chance to open it an open-topped Jeep driven at speed drew up behind it. Chloe stepped back from the cloud of dust it threw up, but before it had even settled Tatiana, wearing a cotton shirt over a tee shirt and shorts, her shiny bell of dark hair pulled back off her make-up-free face in a severe ponytail, jumped out.

Chloe felt the teenager beside her tense and heard her sharp intake of breath, before she stuck out her chin and quavered out defiantly, 'Before you say anything—'

'How could you?' her mother ground out.

'I...' Without warning the youngster's belligerence vanished and she started to sob heartbrokenly. A second later she was in her mother's arms being told everything would be all right. Chin resting on her daughter's head, a shiny-eyed Tatiana shot a look of gratitude in Chloe's direction.

'We are so, so grateful to you, Chloe.'

'It's fine. I'm glad I could help.'

The image of Chloe sniffing into a tissue at the scene in front of her while she blinked hard made something tighten in Nik's chest, but he ignored it and drawled out sarcastically, 'Are you going to cry too?'

'I am not crying!' Chloe snapped back, blowing her nose hard.

'Do you mind travelling back with Nik?' Tatiana asked, glancing at her brother for the first time. 'I could do with talking one to one with this one.' She kissed the top of her daughter's head. 'Alone.'

Chloe minded very much. In fact, the idea of sharing the back seat of the limo with Nik filled her with horror, but she hid her feelings behind a smile and shook her head.

'Actually I don't mind waiting here to catch a lift straight back to the mainland.'

Tatiana looked blank and then shocked. 'You don't think we'd let you go straight back, do you? Heavens, you're here as our guest for as long as you like.'

'I couldn't possibly stay.' Chloe tried to sound firm, but all she sounded was tired as she lifted a hand to her ticcing eyelid.

'Perhaps Chloe has other places to be.' And other people she'd rather be with, he thought sourly, and the silent addition caused the line between his dark brows to deepen.

'You can't fly straight back,' Tatiana argued.

'Not unless she sprouts wings,' Nik inserted drily. 'Marco is refuelling the jet and then heading straight off to Düsseldorf.'

He slid effortlessly into Greek as he added something to Tatiana, who nodded in agreement.

'Well, that settles it, then, you'll stay with us...at least for tonight...to let me say thank you...?'

'But your grandmother is unwell...' Chloe began searching desperately for a legitimate reason to refuse their hospitality, or at least a reason that wasn't, *I really can't be around your brother because I don't want to be reminded of something I want but can't have, and shouldn't even want to begin with!*

It sounded convoluted even in her own head, but then so was her relationship with Nik. Except she didn't have a relationship with Nik. She closed one eye as the eyelid tic started up again.

'She's a lot better.'

'Yaya is a tough old bird,' Nik said gruffly, the warmth in his voice when he spoke of his grandmother unmistakeable.

*And I'm sure there are some serial killers who love their grannies too,* Chloe reminded herself as she fought hard against any lowering of the levels of antagonism that she felt were essential to maintain. Bad enough that she lusted after him, liking him as well would be too, *too* much to take.

'Well, that's settled, you'll follow us,' Tatiana announced.

Chloe, who was pretty sure that she hadn't agreed to anything, not that that seemed to bother anyone in the Latsis family, opened her mouth to protest but Tatiana was telling Eugenie to throw her bag in the back. 'Or, better still, Nik can take the scenic route and show Chloe...oh, no!' Her eyes slid past her brother and her enthusiasm morphed into dismay. 'Get in the car,' she said sharply to her daughter, then, after adding something urgent-sounding in Greek to Nik, she climbed in beside the girl and slipped back into English, saying hastily, 'Sorry, Nik, but I don't want Eugenie to get caught up in this.'

Nik, who had turned to follow the direction his sister was looking, nodded. 'You get going. Chloe, get in the car.'

Tatiana was already starting up the engine and Chloe couldn't help turning round to see what had caused her friend to rush off.

There was a woman approaching them, about fifty feet or so away now, who was by turns running then walking, or rather stumbling, towards them, her uncoordinated gait suggesting she'd been drinking.

Chloe didn't have a clue what was happening, but she was the only one, it seemed. Even the driver, who had murmured something in Greek to Nik and got back behind the wheel after receiving a nod in response, seemed to be in the know, but she did recognise an order when she heard one. She told herself she wouldn't have obeyed him on principle, even if she hadn't been eaten up with curiosity to discover what was going on!

'I said—' Nik began, still not looking at her, but Chloe could feel the tension coming off him in waves. His taut profile looked grey and grim, and the muscles along his clenched jawline were set like iron.

'I heard you, which isn't the same as obeying you,' she said calmly.

He turned his dark head then, flashing her a look of seething impatience, and ground out, 'I really don't have time for this now.'

The woman was close enough now for Chloe to see that she was correct in surmising that the woman was drunk; she could smell the alcohol from yards away. So, it seemed, could Nik, who set his shoulders and turned back with an air of forced resignation as he waited until she was within hearing distance.

'Hello, Helena.'

The woman was probably pretty when she remembered to comb her hair and her eyes weren't lost in black-smudged circles of mascara that had been washed by tears running in dark rivers down her face.

The sound coming from her was half sob, half breathless pant as she walked straight past Chloe, her attention totally focused on Nik, her eyes burning with hatred.

Nik didn't move an inch as the woman staggered up to him, glaring.

'I wake up every morning wishing you were dead!' she slurred. 'I wish I was dead!'

The mixture of venom and despair in her voice sent an ice-cold chill down Chloe's spine but Nik just stood there. What made it all the more bizarre was that he didn't look angry, he looked…sad, compassionate and, most telling of all, guilty.

Chloe's imagination went into overdrive. What had he done to this woman?

'I'm so sorry,' he said finally.

The woman's face screwed up and an anguished high-pitched shriek left her open mouth as she pulled back her arm and aimed a closed-fisted blow that made contact with Nik's cheek.

Chloe gasped in alarm, her hand going to her own cheek, but he just stood there and continued to do so as the woman started to pound his chest with her flailing fists, shrieking hysterically the whole time.

As the frenzied attack showed no sign of abating, although God knew where the woman got the strength from, the shock that had held Chloe immobile abated.

'No!' She wasn't even aware that she'd voiced her protest or had moved forward until Nik looked at her and moved his head in a negative motion.

It was the total absence of anger in his austere, strong-boned face that hit her, that and the profound sadness. It added a deep ache of empathy to the already present confusion and horror—too many layers of emotion for Chloe to comprehend.

His headshake coincided with the woman running out of steam and she finally slumped her head against Nik's chest, weeping in a way that hurt to listen to.

After a moment Nik lifted a tentative hand to her head, smoothing the tangles of hair down in a gentle stroking motion.

'I'll take her.'

Her focus totally on the tableau before her, Chloe hadn't heard the approach of a man wearing a harassed expression. 'Come on, honey, that's it. I didn't know where you'd got to.' The woman lifted her head slightly at the sound of his voice.

'The bastard should be dead!'

For all the reaction Nik showed to this venomous declaration he might as well have been, the skin drawn tight across the prominent bones on his face giving them the appearance of stone.

The stranger took the weeping woman, who reminded Chloe of a puppet whose strings had been severed, and pulled her against him, wrapping a supportive arm around her ribs as he half dragged, half lifted her away from Nik. 'Sorry, you know she doesn't mean it; she doesn't know what she's saying.' The woman continued to weep uncontrollably as she slumped up against him.

The stranger looked from the woman he held to Nik with an expression that brought a lump to Chloe's throat. 'It's not always this bad, but it's particularly hard today...'

Nik nodded, his face still granite.

'She's been drinking all morning. I thought maybe being here with family would help.' He stopped and shook his head. 'Bad idea. I stopped for gas and she must have seen you... I had no idea that you'd be here.'

'Neither did I. It was an unexpected visit. Is there anything I can do...?'

The woman's head lifted at that. 'Haven't you done enough already?' she slurred, before pressing her face back into the man's shoulder as he turned and began to walk away down the road.

Nik watched for a few moments before he looked at Chloe. Some of the rigidity had gone from his tense posture, but not the lines of tension bracketing his mouth or the shadow in his eyes. 'Have you seen enough now?'

She flinched, but didn't react to the unspoken accusation, which was both harsh and unjust, that she had taken some voyeuristic pleasure at the scene she had witnessed.

'Are you all right?' she asked, wincing inside at the crassness of her words, and she wasn't surprised when he just flashed her a look.

The muscles along his taut jaw tensed as he turned away. He didn't want or deserve Chloe's sympathy.

Are you *all right*? she'd asked. Well, he was certainly more all right than the man who would have been thirty-five today if he'd lived. An image floated in his head, of Charlie grinning as he delivered the punchline of one of his terrible jokes, Charlie looking guilty when he explained this would be the last time they worked together because he was letting his lovely Helena finally make an honest man of him.

Nik remembered feeling pleased that he'd managed to

guilt Charlie into one last assignment, though he hadn't succeeded in planting a seed of doubt in his friend's mind when he'd predicted that Charlie wouldn't be able to live without the adrenaline buzz.

*You know when it's time to quit,* Charlie had said.

# CHAPTER EIGHT

CHLOE WAS LEFT standing there when without a word Nik got into the front seat of the car beside the driver. She blew out a breath and for once in her life wished someone would tell her what to do or at least what to think.

A reel of the terrible scene still played in her head. She had only witnessed it and she felt shaken and physically sick; she couldn't begin to imagine what Nik was feeling and she had the distinct impression he wouldn't be telling her any time soon.

She gave her head a tiny shake and slid into the back seat. In the front Nik was speaking to the driver, issuing instructions, she assumed, but she didn't know for sure because it was literally all Greek to her.

Apart from that, they drove in absolute stony silence. A couple of times Chloe cleared her throat to ask how long it would take to reach their destination or for that matter where they were heading but chickened out at the last moment. So silence reigned until about maybe ten minutes into the journey when Nik suddenly spoke in Greek once again.

The driver responded in the same language and pulled onto the side of the road. The car had barely stopped when Nik flung himself out, and, leaving the door open, he strode off into the scrub at the side of the deserted road up an incline, immediately disappearing from view as he went down the other side.

So what did she do now?

Did she sit here and wait, or did she follow him…? She caught the eyes of the driver in the rear-view mirror, and his expression was sympathetic but he just shrugged.

'I think I'll stretch my legs,' she said, not sure he understood her or if he'd try and prevent her from leaving the car.

He didn't.

Grateful her shoes only had moderate heels, she stumbled her way across the steep slope of the rough ground, waking up tiny little things in the undergrowth as she picked out a path between the rocks, following roughly— she hoped—the route she had seen Nik take. The linen trousers she wore were of a loose style that ended mid-calf, protecting most of her legs from the razor-sharp ends of the long tough grass that poked through the rocks. But her calves already ached; the incline was steeper than it looked.

She had lost track of time today but the sun overhead was still high in the sky that was a uniform blue. It was very hot and she became uncomfortably aware of rivulets of sweat trickling down her back. Pausing to rest, she turned her head to make sure that she had not lost sight of the car.

Getting lost really would add the finishing touch to this day. Nik had seemed to vanish from view after only moments, so either he was astonishingly fit or she had somehow gone off course and attacked the slope at a wider angle.

Probably both, she decided, pausing again, this time just below the top of the incline. She ran her tongue over her lips; they felt dry and she was thirsty. Without the crunch of her footsteps, she could make out a distant whooshing sound above the softer constant buzzing of the bees that smothered the sweet-smelling wild thyme that filled the air with a deep sweet fragrance.

She closed her eyes and inhaled.

*What are you doing?* she asked herself wearily. *So you find him—what then? Does he strike you as a man who needs a shoulder to cry on?* Like a wounded animal, he'd gone away to lick his wounds; he clearly wanted privacy and she was going to crash it. It had seemed like a good idea at the time—but *why* exactly?

She puffed out a gusty sigh. This was starting to feel like a very bad idea, but, torn between turning back and pushing on, she hesitated only momentarily before tackling the last few feet of slope.

As she crowned the hill her efforts were rewarded by a view that made her catch her breath. In contrast to the steep slope she had just climbed, the other side was a very gentle incline, the vegetation spare where it grew out of the sandy ground, but she barely noticed as her eyes went to the horseshoe curve of a bay ringed by rocks. Alternating stripes of pebbles and silvery sand ran down to the water. Beyond the gentle waves that frothed white as they broke on the beach, the blue of the sea deepened, interspersed with iridescent swirling areas of deep green and dark turquoise before it met the sky.

The view was so unexpected and so soul-soothingly beautiful that for a long moment all she did was stare, but the moment of spiritual peace shattered into a million shards as her eyes reached the figure standing at the farthest point of the beach before the rocks rose up out of the water.

Nik stood, his tall, remote figure a dark silhouette against the backdrop of bright blue. The strength of the empathetic sympathy that swelled in her chest took her by surprise, and, without pausing to examine it or the need to be with him right now, she began to jog towards him, the downward journey on the smooth, gentle slope far less taxing than the climb up it.

Once she reached the sand she slowed until finally pausing to remove her shoes. Swinging them from the fingers of one hand, she continued slowing as she picked her way across the bands of smooth stones that were sandwiched between the wider bands of powdery sand.

The closer she got to the water, the more she felt the breeze, warm but very welcome as it lifted the damp strands of hair from her neck. She stopped a few feet away from Nik, suddenly unsure what to do next, which seemed to suggest she'd ever known. The thought that she actually knew what she was doing or had any sort of plan when it came to Nik tugged her lips into an ironic, self-mocking smile.

Blind instinct had got her this far and if she had any sense, Chloe reflected, it would take her straight back the way she had come.

She never had had much sense.

'It's very beautiful.'

He didn't react to her comment, so she assumed he already knew she was there. She took a few more steps towards him, in the shade cast by the rocks, which meant it was pleasantly cooler underfoot. But not as cool as standing ankle deep in the water, which Nik was doing in his beautiful handmade leather shoes, although he seemed utterly oblivious.

'Don't worry; I'm not going to ask you if you're all right.'

'Are you moving on to *you probably deserve it*?' he tossed back, thinking grimly that if so, she was right.

Digging his hands deep into the pockets of his tailored trousers, he stared sightlessly in front of him, eyes narrowed at the horizon, trying to remember what it felt like not to carry this constant weight of guilt around with him.

He swivelled around, his short hair catching the breeze as a sudden spurt of stronger wind made it stick up in sexy tufts.

As their eyes connected it struck Chloe with the force of a blow that his expression was exactly the same as the first time she had seen him, dark and tortured. The sight made her heart squeeze in her chest.

The expression he caught on her face stung his pride into painful life, but he didn't want her concern, genuine or otherwise. He didn't deserve concern, and certainly not from her... Hell, life had been easier when she had been filed in his memory banks under the heading of a typical shallow, narcissistic socialite. He had used her once to distract himself from his past and he was doing the same thing now; why didn't she seem able to recognise a lost cause when she saw one?

'No, I don't think you deserved it.' Chloe's first thought had been that she was seeing an ex-lover he'd done the dirty on seeking revenge, and to her shame she had been prepared to be the cheering squad, but the impression had only lasted for seconds as it had almost immediately become obvious that she was seeing something much more complicated.

An expression she couldn't interpret flickered across his face. 'Well, I do.' He flung the words at her like a challenge.

'You must have done something really bad, then,' she said calmly.

A sense of deep self-loathing rushed through him with the force of a forest fire. His chest heaving, he heard a roar inside his skull before the feelings he'd kept locked inside for years finally exploded out. 'I killed a man—my best friend.'

'I'm sorry.'

His head came up with a snap.

'*Sorry!*' he echoed as he began to walk out of the water towards her with slow deliberate steps. Confession was supposed to be good for the soul but he didn't feel good or cleansed; he felt furious with himself for losing control, especially in front of the last person he wanted to see…see what?

The question brought him to a halt when he was six inches away from her, so close that she had actually closed her eyes to shut out the awe-inspiring image he presented.

She could feel the heat of his body through the narrow gap between them but it was nothing compared to the anger and frustration that the air was practically coloured with that rippled off him in almost tangible waves.

He dragged a frustrated hand roughly across his forehead, but as he scanned her face for a clue to what she was thinking his own expression was cloaked. 'Did you hear what I just said?'

'You said that you killed your best friend. I have no idea what actually happened but, as they put people in jail for murder and you are not there, I'm assuming—'

He interrupted her, speaking through clenched teeth. 'He is dead.' His shoulders sagged as the anger drained away leaving a desolate hollowness inside his chest. 'I am here.'

The emptiness in his flat delivery brought an ache to her throat. Watching him through her lashes, Chloe struggled to hide the dangerous rise of emotions that made her chest tight.

'I know, Nik, I'm not deaf or blind.'

The hand he was dragging back and forth through his hair stilled at the mild reproof. He shot her a look and wondered for the tenth time in as many seconds why, if he was going to have some sort of meltdown, he had to do it in front of this woman who did not seem to have any concept of personal boundaries.

'I am not one of your charity projects!' he snarled, the very idea offending his masculine pride deeply.

Taken aback by the outraged charge, she just blinked.

'Has it ever occurred to you that people who put so much of themselves into worthwhile causes are compensating for something that is missing in their own lives?'

Anger at this outrageous statement replaced her bewilderment. Face flushed, she compressed her lips and arched a brow. 'Let me guess what you think is missing in my life—a man,' she drawled. 'Why do all men assume that they are essential for a woman's happiness and fulfilment? If there is anything missing in my life I'll get myself a dog. They're far more reliable.'

Eyelids half lowered so that all she could see was a glitter of dark brown, he let the silence that developed between them stretch out taut before breaking it with a thoughtful, 'I obviously touched a nerve there.'

He'd managed to change the subject from his own trauma, she realised, which she was assuming had been his intention all along. 'Your friend is dead and I'm sorry. You might feel responsible, you might *be* responsible in some way, I have no idea, but I do know for definite that you didn't kill anyone.'

'How can you possibly know that?' he jeered. 'You don't know me.'

She found herself wondering if anyone did. Did he push the world away or was it just her? 'Who was that woman?' she asked quietly.

He turned to look at the sea again. 'Her name is Helena and she was engaged to Charlie, my best friend.'

'Do you mind if I sit down?' Without waiting for him to respond, she brushed a piece of silvered driftwood to one side with a foot, set down her shoes and sat down on the sand, stretching her long legs in front of her, crossing them at the ankle.

Nik turned as she was leaning back on her hands, just as the breeze lifted her hair, blowing it across her face before it settled in a fine silky mesh down her back except for a few errant strands that stuck to her face. Wrinkling her nose, she pursed her lips and huffed them away.

There was something about her beauty that could touch him in a way he hadn't known he was capable of even at a time like this. He made an effort to resurrect a scowl but gave up on the attempt, deciding instead to sit down beside her.

'Charlie was a cameraman, the best there was. People often forget when they see some correspondent standing there in the middle of a gun battle that there's a man behind the camera too, taking the same risks without the same recognition. We'd worked together for two years in the sort of environment where…well, let's just say that you get to see the best and worst of people.'

Chloe glanced sideways at his face…and wondered what he was seeing as he stared out to sea. For a while there was nothing but the hissing sound of the waves breaking a few feet away, and she had the impression he had forgotten she was there.

When he finally spoke his deep, strong voice held a rusty crack.

'He met Helena through me. Her family are part of the London Greek expat community too, but like us they have relatives who still live here on the island. When I was a kid staying with my grandparents I used to hang around with her brothers. That was one of them with her back at the airport—Andreos. Helena used to tag along with us,' he recalled. 'A nice kid.'

And the nice kid had grown up to be a beautiful young woman with everything to live for, except now she didn't want to live.

'She and Charlie hit it off straight away. I was surprised as they were total opposites. Charlie was an extrovert and she was thoughtful, quiet and...' He swallowed hard, the muscles in his brown throat working.

It really hurt her to see him struggle. 'So it was a whirlwind romance?'

'Actually more of a slow burner,' Nik recalled. 'They had an on-off thing that lasted eighteen months or so, the sort of thing that often fizzles out. But then something changed... I don't know what it was, but they got engaged.'

She watched as he silently wrestled with the emotions inside him. Finally, she prompted softly, 'You were surprised.'

He turned his head, his dark eyes glittering with self-contempt as he contradicted her. 'I was irritated. We were a team and Charlie had announced that he was quitting and moving to a safe job where there was no risk of being kidnapped or shot.

'It was me who persuaded him to take that one last assignment together. I was convinced that he'd realise that he couldn't survive without the adrenaline rush, that he'd resent Helena if he gave up a life he loved for her. Oh, I was a *really* caring friend.' Nik squeezed his eyes closed, still seeing Charlie's dead eyes, his nostrils flaring at the remembered metallic iron scent of blood. 'So it did turn out to be his last assignment after all, and he was only there because of me.'

Chloe swallowed the lump in her throat and turned her head to hide the tears that filled her eyes before picking up a handful of sand and letting the silver particles slide through her fingers, watching them vanish into the billions of identical grains. Risking a look at him through her lashes, she saw his expression was completely remote as though he'd retreated to another place entirely.

She didn't attempt to react to his words until she had full control of her emotions again. Nik didn't want her tears or her sympathy; he'd made that obvious. The only thing he wanted from her was her body, which rather begged the question as to why she was getting involved with his problems, seeing as it was the one thing she couldn't give him.

'What happened was a tragedy.' She winced at the triteness of her comment. 'But how exactly is it your fault?'

He vented a hard laugh and looked at her incredulously. 'Have you listened to a word I said?' He still didn't know why he'd said those words—any of them.

He was already regretting it.

He was a private man living in a world where people were tripping over themselves to expose their innermost thoughts and feelings, mostly for public scrutiny. You couldn't turn on a television or a computer, or open a newspaper, without finding some celebrity *revealing all*, but the idea of turning your personal tragedies and failings into entertainment for the masses made his blood run cold.

Getting to his feet, he brushed the sand off his clothes

and stood there looking down at her. 'Tatiana will be wondering what has happened to us.'

Chloe uncrossed her legs and raised herself gracefully to her feet. 'Do you think you're honouring your friend in some way by beating yourself up for being alive? The way you talk about him, it doesn't make it sound as though your friend Charlie would have approved.'

'Helena might disagree.'

'Come on, you're an intelligent man—it doesn't take a professional to see that the poor woman needs help. She's attacking you because she wants someone to blame.' She shook her head in disbelief as he turned and walked away. 'Nik!' Cursing softly under her breath, she picked up her shoes from the sand and ran after him. 'Fine,' she said, falling breathlessly into step beside him. 'Deal with it by ignoring the problem. That always works, doesn't it? It's very adult of you!' How the hell could you help a man who was too stubborn to admit he needed it?

He stopped and swung around to face her, feeling a twisting feeling in his chest as he looked down into her angry face. 'I did not invite you into my head, so stay out!'

'Or what?' she charged, pitying the woman who one day actually wanted to reach him, whose heart ached to help him.

He reached out and cupped a hand around the back of her head, drawing her up onto her toes until their lips were a whisper apart. 'Or this.'

Her gasp of shock was lost in the warmth of his mouth as it came crashing down hard on hers. He kissed her like a man starving for the taste, kissed her as though he'd drain her. One big hand slid down the curve of her back, coming to rest on the smooth curve of her bottom, dragging her up against the grinding hardness of his erection.

His free hand moved to the back of her head to hold her face up to his as the kiss continued on and on until her head was spinning.

Her body arched against him as her shoes fell from her nerveless fingers. Mouths still sealed, they took a few staggering steps together as the ferocity of their desire intensified. Chloe's knees were on the point of buckling when without warning he suddenly let her go.

She slid down to the sand and sat there, arms wrapped around herself as she looked up at him, her big eyes wide and shocked. Bleeding control from every nerve ending, Nik's hands clenched by his sides… He wanted to shed the pain, lose himself inside her—but he knew he would be using her in exactly the same way he'd used other women…using sex to gain a few moments' oblivion.

Why couldn't he bring himself to use Chloe?

'*That's* my way of dealing with it, *agape mou,*' he told her harshly, staring at the pouting line of her lips, which were still swollen from his kisses. 'So if you're feeling sorry for me and fancy a bit of pity sex…?'

Even as she winced at the deliberate crudity of his suggestion, shameful excitement clenched low in her belly.

'It was just a thought,' he drawled.

She watched him stalk away, wondering how anyone managed to look rock-hard, tough and vulnerable all at the same time, but then he was a man of massive contradictions. Her energy levels felt as though they'd moved into negative territory as she began to slowly slog her way through the sand after him. It wasn't until the car came into view with Nik standing beside it looking impatient that she realised what the tight feeling in her chest was— fear. She had never felt more scared in her life, which was saying something.

She couldn't be in love with Nik. She lifted her chin in defiance at the idea… She *refused* to be in love with him.

As she approached he opened the back door for her.

She tipped her head in acknowledgment and murmured sarcastically, 'What a gentleman,' before slamming the door behind her just in case he thought he was going to ride in the back with her.

# CHAPTER NINE

'DO YOU LIKE IT?'

'It's beautiful,' Chloe said honestly as she walked around the room that Eugenie had guided her to. 'What a view,' she exclaimed, walking over to the open French doors. Three steps away was the infinity pool and beyond that the sea.

'It used to be a little tiny cottage, and Granny was born here,' the teenager confided. 'She was poor. That must be awful, I think. When she married Grandpa he wanted to knock it down but she wouldn't let him so he built around it. There wasn't any beach here then, so he brought the sand and made one.'

'What about the big place on the hill?' It had looked Venetian and just gorgeous set against a backdrop of pines.

'Oh, we own that too. Grandpa bought it but Yaya wouldn't live in it and he preferred modern so...' She gave a shrug that made Chloe think of her uncle. 'It's pretty much falling down now.'

'That's sad,' Chloe said, glancing through the doors of a walk-in closet, realising that she didn't have even so much as a toothbrush with her.

The girl seemed to read her thoughts. 'Don't worry. Mum will organise you some stuff.'

'No, really—'

'It's fine. She has closets full of samples.' She looked at Chloe with envy. 'They wouldn't fit anyone else here. Are you sure you won't join us for dinner?'

Chloe resisted the pleading tone and gave a firm shake of her head, adding, 'I'm really whacked.' She escorted Eugenie to the door and closed it behind her reluctant-to-leave guest.

She released a sigh and leaned back against the wall, willing the images that were flashing through her head to stop or at least slow down because they made her dizzy.

Finally summoning the energy to kick off her shoes, she flopped onto the bed and lay there staring at the fan that was whirring silently above her head.

She had pleaded exhaustion when she had been given the option of a tray in her room, which suggested she looked as bad as she felt. The bone-deep weariness felt as if it were crushing her; even lifting a hand to her head was an effort, as was closing her eyes. But when she'd managed it, opening them again was just not an option.

She suspected her weariness was as much emotional as physical. Lack of sleep was the reason, she decided, unwilling to admit the truth even to herself.

She touched her lips, a silent sigh rippling through her body as she remembered the moment Nik's eyes had dropped to her mouth and she'd known he was thinking about kissing her... Had he been able to feel how much she wanted him to? Oh, God, why was she even wasting her time thinking about it? It was just a damned kiss; there was nothing deep and meaningful about it!

She sighed, thinking, *I'll get up in a minute and shower the day and the memories away...* There was no hurry.

* * *

Fighting her way out of sleep was like fighting her way through layers of gauze, convinced when she finally broke through the veil of sleep that she had heard someone crying out.

She lay there listening but it was silent except for the sounds of the night coming in through the open door.

Night!

She sat up abruptly, looking around the room. It was dark but not inky black, as the sky outside the door was tinged faintly with red. She reached for the lamp switch and found it, illuminating the room and revealing a tray on a table, the food covered by domes.

She swung her legs over the side of the bed and the first thing her glance lighted on was a full-length silk kaftan hanging on a hook of the door to the bathroom. She smiled as she got stiffly to her feet. She picked up her phone and glanced at the time, her eyes widening as she saw it was five-thirty in the morning!

She picked up one of the domes and looked at the food, but she was not hungry enough to be tempted by the sad, cold remains of what had, she had no doubt, been a delicious meal.

There were more clothes neatly folded and stacked on the shelves in the wardrobe and hanging on padded hangers. Tatiana had clearly crept in while she was asleep like a petite Greek Santa. She yawned and stretched, wondering about Greek Christmas traditions.

She spent a long time in the shower and emerged feeling half human. Laying out a towel on the bed, she sat down and began rubbing the oil one of her physiotherapists had recommended into the tight tissues of her scars with light but firm strokes.

Maybe its effects were just a placebo but it smelt good

and, while it was no magic cure-all, her skin always felt more supple after she'd applied it. She had got into the habit of carrying it in her handbag.

She waited for it to dry before she put on the kaftan, enjoying the feel of the silk against her skin. She lifted an arm and performed a swishing motion, smiling. Tatiana really was talented. Drawn by the smells and sounds of early morning, she wandered to the open door and pulled aside the mosquito curtain that someone had pulled across while she slept.

Eyes closed, she breathed in deeply before she walked out, the soft scented breeze blowing the kaftan against her body. A tiny lizard disturbed by her tread emerged from a crack in the stone and vanished beneath the glossy, well-trimmed shrubbery.

The swimming pool lit by underwater lights that reflected the mosaic tiles drew her like a magnet; she loved water. She'd learnt to swim at school and if she had been prepared to put in the sort of dedication that involved a relentless early morning training schedule and no social life she might have been able to compete at a high level.

Physical ability and natural talent were no good unless you had the dedication that went with them and Chloe didn't...but she really loved to swim. Apart from the times she had stayed with her sister, as camera lenses and shocked stares were really not an issue in the royal palace, she had not ventured into the water since the accident.

She liked to think that one day she would be brave enough to swim in a public pool and not care about the stares, but that day had not yet come.

Walking to the edge, she hitched the folds of silk around her knees and sat down, dangling her feet in the warm water, thinking about the lovely feeling of it on her skin.

It was tempting to go in for a swim, it really was... Who was around to see?

Nik had been swimming lengths for ten minutes, pushing his body to the limit in an attempt to wash away the personal devils left in his head after the nightmare had visited him yet again. He neared the wall at the deep end, flipped over and had lifted his head to gulp in air when he saw Chloe approach the pool through a watery haze.

He paused, his head just breaking the surface as he trod water, the shimmering image solidifying. He was unable to take his eyes off her as she walked towards the water, the thin floor-length robe she wore blowing tight against her, outlining every supple curve of her long, luscious body.

She obviously wasn't wearing a stitch underneath.

The sound of blood drumming in his ears became deafening as in his head he saw her opening the garment and slipping it off, then standing there naked on the side before diving in... All she actually did was trail her toes in the water, pretty tame by most standards, but Nik felt his dormant libido once more kick into life—hard.

He took a deep breath and slid silently down under the surface of the water.

Her dreamy thoughts drifted as she continued to inscribe circles in the water with her toes.

The sheer unexpectedness of the sudden tug on her foot drew a shrill shriek from her throat. She pulled against the pressure and scooted back, fighting against the restraint and kicking out wildly.

There was a grunt of pain followed by a curse and she was suddenly free. She had curled both legs up protectively against her body when Nik's sleek dark head appeared, water streaming down his face.

'What the hell did you think you were doing? You nearly gave me a heart attack!' she accused shakily.

'I was swimming…it's good; come in and join me.'

The invitation sent a slam of hormonal heat through her body. She shook her head, her heart thudding like a metronome as she stared at him.

'Fair enough.' It took him two lazy strokes to reach the side. 'Then I'll join you.' Hands flat on the mosaic tiles, he casually heaved himself out of the pool, pausing for a moment on the balls of his feet before straightening up to his full impressive height.

Chloe had no control over her stare, and her skin prickled with heat as her helpless gaze travelled up the length of his long legs, taking in the ridges of his flat belly and broad, hair-roughened chest. His shoulders were muscle packed and powerful but he wasn't bulky. There was a streamlined strength to him, no excess flesh at all to blur the symmetry. Each individual muscle stood out defined and perfect beneath the surface of his gleaming golden skin.

Her eyes reached his face and his white grin flashed, making him look like a very smug fallen angel as he lifted one hand and rubbed it hard across his hair, causing more water to stream down his face.

He tilted his head to one side in an enquiring attitude. 'Sure I can't tempt you?' asked her personal embodiment of temptation, the gleam in his eyes suggesting that this was no secret to him.

Even though it was frustrating it was also true—she had zero control over the colour that rushed to her cheeks—but she refused to drop her gaze, or was it she couldn't escape the grip of his black, heavy-lidded stare?

Her insides clenched as she ran her tongue across the outline of her dry lips.

'No, you can't,' she lied, struggling to inject a note of amusement into her response. 'But don't let me stop you.' Hearing the quiver of something near to desperation in her own voice, she half turned and gave an elaborate yawn. 'I was just going back inside.'

He reached for a towel that was slung over a chair, rubbing it over his dripping hair, then blotting the moisture off his face. 'You really should take a swim.' His eyes went to the wet hair that was slicked back to reveal her smooth, high forehead and perfect pure profile. 'Or have you already?'

She lifted a self-conscious hand, dragging it down the damp surface of her wet hair. 'I showered.'

He swallowed, the muscles in his brown throat visibly working, a nerve spasmodically clenching in his lean cheek as his darkened eyes drifted slowly over her face, then down over the soft curves of her lush body outlined beneath the folds of iridescent fabric, his imagination peeling away the fabric, seeing the water streaming down her smooth skin.

It took Chloe a few moments to realise that the noise she could hear was her own breathing, as she struggled to breathe through the sexual tension that hung in the air.

She wasn't sure that Nik was breathing at all. He just stood there, the bands of dull colour running along the slashing angles of his cheekbones emphasising their razor-edged prominence as the moments ticked away. Each passing second made her heart beat faster until she could feel the thuds vibrating throughout her entire body.

'I... I need to go.' Her voice sounded as though it was coming from a long way away.

'Why?'

'I need to book my flight.'

'It's six a.m.'

'Online.'

'Eugenie will be disappointed; she was looking forward to showing you the sights.'

'I need to get back.' There was a hint of a plea in her voice.

He shrugged and looped the towel around his middle, drawing her attention once again to his flat, ribbed belly and the thin directional line of dark hair that vanished into the waistband of the black shorts he wore. 'Are you sure you won't join me for a swim? It'll take the edge off it.'

She didn't make the mistake of asking what *it* was.

How would he react, she wondered, if she pulled the kaftan open and stood there scars and all? *Why are you even asking the question?* she asked herself.

*He's not interested in your heart or soul; he only wants the beautiful body—or the one he thinks you still have.*

'I don't have a swimsuit.'

His eyes dropped. 'You've never skinny-dipped?'

She stiffened and lowered her lashes over an expression that tugged his dark brows into a straight interrogative line above his hooded stare... *Sadness* seemed an inexplicable reaction for her to have.

'Are you afraid of the water?' he asked gently.

Her eyes slid longingly over the still surface of the pool, but she shook her head.

'Do you often swim at this time of the morning? Are you in training or something?' She'd only been changing the subject, but now that she'd thrown the idea out there she found it wasn't actually a struggle to see him competing in a triathlon or something; he had the body, the fitness levels and undoubtedly the competitive streak it took for such an endurance event.

'No, I usually run.' He bent and picked up a second towel before rubbing his still-wet hair vigorously with it.

'So you are in training?'

He dropped the towel. 'I don't sleep.'

The confession evoked a rush of sympathy in Chloe. Midway through her hospitalisation, when the heavy doses of analgesia she'd been prescribed for pain had been reduced, she'd suffered badly from insomnia. Though it was not a time she thought about often, choosing instead to focus on the fact she had survived, the experience had left her wary of taking even an aspirin and she'd gained a personal appreciation of the negative impact insomnia could have on a person's daily life.

'I suppose it's hard to switch off sometimes.' *Especially when you have chosen to carry around guilt the size of a planet... Not your problem, Chloe,* she reminded herself, rejecting the stab of empathy that made her chest tighten. People who deserved sympathy were those who actually tried to do something about a problem. 'I settle for warm milk—not very cutting edge, I know, but that usually does the trick for me.'

He gave a sudden hard laugh. 'I don't want to sleep.'

'You mean you don't *need* much sleep?' He fitted the profile of the driven alpha type you generally associated with surviving on two or three hours a night.

'I mean I have nightmares.' The hand he was dragging across his face stilled, shock flickering in his hooded gaze as he asked himself why the hell he had just told her that.

His nightmares were something he had never discussed with anyone. Did he suffer from some form of post-traumatic stress disorder? He was sure there were any number of so-called experts who would be happy to tell him. In Nik's view the label didn't matter. Sharing was not his style and the idea of being an object of pity was something that he rejected on a visceral level.

Charlie was dead because of him and no label was going to change that. He didn't want to feel better... He didn't *deserve* to feel better, he accepted that, but the nightmares were a punishment too far.

She blew out a long fatalistic sigh. She knew that she was issuing an invitation to have her head bitten off but she couldn't bring herself to do *nothing. Story of your life, Chloe.*

'So do you want to talk about it?'

He turned his head and glared at her. 'Can you turn off the empathy for a minute? That's not what I want from you.'

Chloe held her ground. 'You're not responsible for what happened, Nik. Charlie made his own decisions.'

'How the hell can you say that? I told you...' He stopped, his eyes narrowing over an expression of angry bewilderment. Why *had* he told her when he hadn't told anyone else? He didn't like that he couldn't answer the question. He was at her side in three strides, his hand closing around her upper arms as he dragged her into him until their bodies collided. 'Why do you have to be different?'

The emotions pouring off him made her dizzy, or was that the contact with his hard, lean body? The sexual pulse emanating from him and the feverish glitter in his dark eyes made her head spin.

His eyes stayed open and connected with her own as his lips moved across her parted lips, the contact a mere whisper, the progress agonisingly slow.

She shuddered and sank deeper into the suffocating excitement that caused her breath to come in short, shivery little gasps. His face blurred before she closed her eyes and the ache of hunger low in her pelvis dragged a sob from her aching throat as she whispered fiercely.

'Please!'

The hoarse, hungry plea snapped whatever shred of control he retained as, with a moan deep in his own throat, Nik plunged his tongue into her mouth, plundering the warm recesses. The kiss grew wild, teeth clashed, tongues tasting with an escalating passion.

Rising up on her toes, Chloe put her arms around his neck to hold on for grim death. She could still hear alarm bells ringing but they were almost drowned out by the excited clamour of her own heartbeat. Her fingers dug into the smooth muscled skin of his shoulders and back as she pulled him closer, craving the connection of their bodies.

He'd still been clinging to the idea that making love to her was some sort of therapy to drive his devils away, but that illusion burned away the moment his hands began to move over her body, exploring the soft curves.

This wasn't therapy, this was survival—he felt as though his life depended on this. He *needed* this; he *needed* her. No, it was just sex, he amended as he cupped one warm breast in his hand and held it, his thumb rubbing across the engorged peak as he kissed his way up the curve of her neck.

'You make me want you!' he growled, thinking that all she had to do was breathe and he was out of his mind with lust. 'I just want to feel your skin on mine. I have to kiss and taste every inch of you.'

*What was she doing? Your skin on mine, he'd said...* In her mind's eye she suddenly saw the puckered flesh of her thigh and imagined the shocked disgust on his face when he discovered it. And she couldn't bear it.

*'No...no!'* She pushed hard against him and his arms fell away. He stepped back, his chest lifting and falling

dramatically as he appeared to struggle to draw enough air into his lungs.

'What is happening here, Chloe?'

She gave a tight little smile and thought, *I'm dying.* 'Nothing is happening. I just…changed my mind.'

'You changed your mind?' The lines of colour along his cheekbones stood out starkly against his blanched, sweaty pallor. He looked like a man in shock and he felt like a man in purgatory!

She took a deep, controlling breath. 'You come with too much baggage for me… I like to keep things simple.'

His head went back as though she'd struck him; he was aching and hurting and mad as hell. She thought he was some sort of emotional cripple who needed taking care of and she didn't want the job! The injury to his pride was almost as painful as the frustration that raged through his body. 'It's only sex, *agape mou*; I'm not asking you to marry me.'

She knew it was irrational to let the words hurt, but they did anyway. 'Maybe, but *just sex* can get complicated.'

'I'm a man of simple needs.'

She gave a bitter smile. 'You don't need to tell me that. As I recall you didn't even manage to say a simple goodbye…' She regretted the words even before she registered the speculation in his eyes and rushed into further speech. 'I really think you should talk to someone qualified, about the nightmares, I mean. It's good that you don't drink to excess now, but the way you were that night…'

'The night we had sex, you mean.' He saw her flinch and was glad; she deserved to flinch after her harsh rejection of him just now. 'There hadn't been any nightmares that night because I hadn't been to sleep.'

There was a beat of silence before a look of shocked comprehension slid across her face, taking with it any trace of colour that had been there. By the time she breathed again even her lips were bloodless and the only colour in her entire face was the burning blue of her eyes.

'Charlie's death had just happened, hadn't it?' But it wasn't a question... Suddenly it all made sense: the darkness in him, the combustible quality of their chemistry, the driving need of his lovemaking—he'd been trying to burn away the pain of his memories in the fire of passion.

He tipped his head in acknowledgment, the weight in his chest painful as he looked at her standing there, frail and defenceless. Wasn't there already enough guilt in his life?

'You used me.' Anger and hurt shimmered through her and she didn't care if she was being rational; she didn't feel rational.

'I was too tired to fight you off,' he shot back.

Chloe flushed. At what point had she thought he would *ever* let her in? 'You really are a bastard.'

He didn't deny it. How could he? It was true. She turned away. 'Where are you going?' He had to clamp his lips tight over the word *stay*! He had never begged a woman in his life, and he wasn't about to start now.

'Going?' She turned back and lifted her chin. 'As far away from you as I can get!' she flung childishly. 'And who knows? If I'm lucky I might find a man who is not afraid to admit he's not perfect.'

'*Agape mou*, you're not looking for a man, you're looking for a cause!' he sneered contemptuously.

'Maybe I am, but you're a *lost* cause,' she flung back. 'You'll never have a future until you forgive yourself for the past. And you don't want me, you want a memory of something perfect... Well, I'm not that. I'm...' Breathing hard, she fought her way out of the kaftan, ripping the silk as she tore it off her body and stood there naked in the light of the breaking dawn.

He sucked in a deep breath, his eyes moving down over her body. She watched his face and saw the exact moment when he reached the area where the skin was badly scarred, saw the shock and horror he couldn't conceal.

That tiny flame of hope died right then and there.

'You see, I'm not what you need. I'm not perfect any more.'

She had no idea how she managed to walk the few steps back to her room, oblivious to the fact he had followed her.

# CHAPTER TEN

THE VIOLENCE WITH which she'd slammed the door behind her made it swing back open, but she seemed oblivious to that as he stepped over the torn silk robe that lay crumpled on the floor.

It took him a few dazed seconds to label the emotion that broke loose inside him as tenderness when his gaze lifted to the slim figure standing there, staring blankly straight ahead like a beautiful, flawless marble statue... Except she was not stone, she was blood and flesh and nerve endings, and the flaw on her body that stood out only emphasised how stunning she really was.

He could only imagine what was going through her mind. This woman had more guts in her little finger than a regiment of marines.

'Haven't you seen enough?' she asked, staring at a point over his left shoulder. If he hadn't, she certainly had!

She would never forget that look of horror in his eyes.

Every resource he had was needed to retain his control, but he was straining at the leash so hard he could barely form the word. 'No!'

Her eyes flew to his face as he walked towards her, the fierce tenderness in his eyes making her tummy flip and her throat tighten, as she had no defence against it.

'But...'

'I want to do more than look at you,' he growled out, lifting a big hand to curve his fingers around one side of her face. 'And I think we can do better than just sex!' he declared with arrogant confidence. Holding her startled gaze, he bent his head, closing his eyes only when their mouths were sealed together.

When he raised his head they were both breathing hard, her eyes were bright, her skin was feverishly hot, and every skin cell on her body was bursting with painful awareness.

'Let's even things up a bit, shall we?' he suggested, stepping away but only far enough to slide his wet shorts over his hips.

She swallowed, her eyes dropping to watch his actions, helpless to resist the desire that flowed through her as she observed how the lowering of the fabric revealed the level of his arousal. He flashed a grin at her, but his features were hard and fierce as he held her eyes.

'Come here!' he demanded.

She did and he took her hand, directing it straight onto his groin and curling her fingers around the hardness of his erection. 'That is what looking at you does to me.'

'But… I'm not…'

'You're perfect to me…and you are perfect for me.'

At the stark declaration the muscles deep inside her fluttered and the rapid rise of desire swept over her like a wave, wiping away the last shreds of her self-consciousness. As she tightened her fingers experimentally over his crotch, excitement swirled through her.

'Amazing!' she murmured.

He gave a low, sexy rumble of laughter that made the hairs on the nape of her neck tingle.

Nik caught hold of her hands, raised them to his lips and pressed kisses into each curling palm before lowering his mouth to hers once again.

The kiss began as a slow, sensual tender exploration and then suddenly it became something else, his tongue driving deeper inside her mouth and eliciting an explosion of raw need and desperation as teeth clashed and tongues collided. Chloe moaned deep and raised herself up on her toes, gasping as her aching, sensitised breasts flattened against his iron-hard chest.

By the time they broke apart, they were both breathing as though they'd just crossed the marathon finishing line, and he hooked a hand behind her neck, sliding his fingers into her hairline, the fingertips gently massaging the skin there.

Then he kissed the swan curve of her neck and Chloe's head fell back in rapture, her eyes squeezed closed on a long sigh that became a groan as his hand claimed first one quivering breast and then the other, stroking then kneading... Her head fell back further to allow him greater access, her spine arching back, supported by the iron strength of the arm across her ribs.

Her passion-glazed blue eyes flickered open as he scooped her up as though she weighed nothing and walked towards the bed.

She stroked his face, touching his mouth, his fascinating, pleasure-giving mouth, thinking that she honestly wouldn't have cared if he had laid her down on the floor and taken her there and then... The thought was both shocking and incredibly exciting to her.

As he strode towards the bed, although she wasn't small or delicate he made her feel both, yet at the same time powerful and strong.

He laid her down on the tumbled sheets and stood there looking down at her, nostrils flared, breathing hard, each breath lifting his ribcage.

His body was hard and tanned, warm, bone, sinew

and muscle all so perfect that the desire low in her belly clutched hard as she stared at him, unable to look away.

'You're beautiful,' she whispered. 'Perfect.' Her eyes suddenly filled with tears as she choked out, 'I wish I still was for you too—'

The rush of emotion he felt when he interpreted the expression in her eyes was shocking in its intensity.

She was grieving.

His expression was both stern and tender as he came down beside her, lowering his long body so that they lay thigh to thigh.

'Listen to me. You are beautiful.'

She gave a teary smile, loving him so much it hurt. 'Inside, maybe.'

'Everywhere,' he contradicted. 'Inside and out. And I want to love every part of you. You have lost something, I know, but let me give you something to fill the space…' He took her hand and laid it on his chest where she could feel the heavy thud of his heartbeat, strong and steady. She could feel it vibrating through her own body; it was as if they were one…but she craved an even more intimate joining.

'I want you,' she said simply.

His eyes darkened in response to the husky plea. 'Then, *agape mou*, you shall have me.'

Arms braced above her head either side, he leaned down and kissed her, and she sighed into his mouth, eager for his taste, wanting to fill her senses with it. The heat was searing and she whimpered as she was swept away on a tidal wave of primitive need.

The erotic exploration of tongue against tongue continued as he lowered his body beside her and turned her onto her side to face him. He lifted his mouth from hers, but only to kiss his way down her neck and then over the quivering mounds of her breasts.

A keening cry escaped her lips at the first brush of his tongue over first one nipple and then the other, then when he took one into his mouth and sucked on it sensuously she gasped.

Her damp nipples continued to ache from his ministrations as he slid lower, his tongue leaving a wet trail over the slight mound of her belly while his fingers moved into the soft curls at the apex of her legs, stroking the damp folds gently and then parting them until he found the tight nub nestling inside.

She was so focused on the new, agonisingly blissful sensations he was creating that she didn't realise at first where he was kissing.

She stiffened, rejection making her eyes fly wide open, hating that he was touching the ugly scarred tissue on her thigh, imagining the disgust he had to be feeling. She didn't want him to have to pretend to be enjoying it. 'No!'

'Yes!' he insisted.

For the space of a heartbeat their eyes connected, and she was the first to look away.

Quivering but quiescent now, she lay there as he gently kissed the damaged skin, her face wet with silent tears that slid unnoticed down her face.

'You can't want to do that.'

Her broken whisper felt like a tight fist around his heart. In response, he loosed a low growl and dragged himself up her body until they were face to face. Holding her gaze, he took her hand and curled her fingers around the hard, silky shaft of his erection. His whole body was trembling with need as she stroked him, breathing in the male musk of his warm body.

She looked into his eyes and the desire blazing there burnt away her last doubts and inhibitions; she suddenly felt free.

Kissing her passionately once again, Nik pulled her on top of him and held her there, his hands curved over her bottom, continuing to kiss her into mindless submission until he finally rolled them both over, reversing their position.

Lying beneath him, Chloe gave herself over to the sensations bombarding her. She surrendered to the feelings, as she surrendered to him.

Then he parted her legs and she held her breath and released it in a low, slow sigh when he finally slid into her. She grabbed his hips, her back arching to deepen the pressure, wanting more.

With a groan he obeyed, giving her everything he'd got.

'Put your legs around me, Chloe.'

She did and he sank deeper into her, each strong movement of him inside her sending her deeper into herself, into him. It became one and the same, and they were both at the core of a firestorm, and when it broke the effect on every nerve cell in her body was electric!

She turned her head on the pillow, where beside her Nik lay gasping for air, his chest heaving and the sweat on his skin cooling.

She began to worry that he was cooling towards her because he suddenly seemed so far apart from her, but before the fear could take root he reached out and dragged her against him, as close as possible.

'What are you doing all the way over there?' he asked, propping his chin on the top of her hair-rumpled head as he pulled up a sheet to cover them both.

'Does it still hurt?' he asked quietly when they were both lying still.

She sat up then, dragging the sheet up to her chin, and looked down at him. 'My leg?'

He nodded.

'Only when I laugh... No, seriously, not really, it's kind of numb because the nerve endings were pretty damaged.'

He was pretty sure that her matter-of-fact delivery covered a world of hurt and pain.

'The skin can get tight sometimes.' She reached out and took a bottle from the bedside table. 'If it does, I usually massage this stuff into it.'

'Were you in hospital for a long time?' The image of her lying alone in a hospital bed enduring such pain produced a fresh surge of protectiveness in him.

'Longer than expected, because the grafts didn't take. There was an infection so they had to start all over again. That's why I'm not going back.'

He stiffened. 'They want you to?'

She nodded. 'They have offered me another op, but that's what they said last time...'

'Shouldn't you listen to expert advice?'

'The surgeon says he *might* be able to improve the appearance, but there are no guarantees, and I've had enough of being poked and prodded.'

The way she said it, the defiance in her tone, made his throat ache with emotion, and his arms tightened around her narrow ribs as he rocked her against him.

'But wouldn't it be worth it if they could improve it?' he said against her neck.

She pulled away, her expression wary. 'I still wouldn't be perfect, and it's not about other people, it's about *me*. *I* have to be able to look in the mirror and know I'm still me...' she pressed a hand to her breasts '...inside.'

He watched the tears slide down her cheeks and felt as

if someone had reached a hand into his chest and pulled out his heart. 'Don't cry, *agape mou*.' He smoothed down her hair with a hand and pulled her back into his arms.

Nik felt regret when he saw the warm rays of sunlight filtering through the blinds, certain to wake Chloe up. The irony of his dismay was not lost on Nik, as for a long time he hadn't been able to wait until he could get out of bed.

But morning was already well established now, which meant that he'd have to let her go and lose the incredible sense of peace and *rightness* he'd felt holding her, a peace that had been better than the sleep his body craved, sleep that he had denied himself out of fear that in the grip of a nightmare he might hurt her. It was a fear with foundation, as there were reported incidents of men suffering from PTSD acting out their nightmares and injuring their partners in their sleep.

If he hurt Chloe, even unconsciously, he knew it would kill him.

The time had come to get up, but on the plus side the bright sunlight made it possible for him to study the face on the pillow beside him. Half obscured by the tangle of silky blonde hair, she lay with one arm across his chest and the other tucked under her head like a pillow. He could make out the fact that her eyelashes fanned out lush and curving against her smooth cheek.

If anyone had told him before yesterday that he would say a woman's name just because he wanted, no, *needed* to hear it he would have laughed them out of the building and yet...

'*Chloe.*'

It was barely a whisper but she must have sensed it because she stirred, whimpering a little and shifting restlessly, then, eyes still closed, she shouted, 'No!' She opened her eyes suddenly, and blinked as the haziness vanished. 'I was dreaming...' she whispered sleepily.

'It sounded like a nightmare.'

'I forgot about my leg and had put on shorts, which is silly because I never forget...' she murmured sleepily. 'People were laughing and pointing at my scars...'

Nik flinched inside. 'I won't let anyone laugh,' he promised fiercely.

Chloe smiled happily as he turned onto his side and pulled her to him, running a hand in long soothing strokes down her back again and again until her breathing evened out once more.

It was a long time since he had spent more than an hour or so in bed with a woman, partly because he didn't want anyone to witness his nightmares. It was ironic, really, that the nightmares this time had been Chloe's.

*You don't have exclusive rights on nightmares, Nik.*

The memory of her pathetic whimpers cut right to his heart, and he kissed her forehead gently, pleased that her breathing was now soft and easy.

She bore her scars so bravely but how many times had she lifted her chin and pretended not to care...as she had with him earlier this morning? Carefully he leaned across her and pressed the phone that lay on the bedside table, so that the time appeared; it was already nearly ten a.m.

His throat was dry and the glass of water remained out of reach.

He moved, sliding a hand from under her, careful not to disturb her, and levered himself from the bed. Walking through to the kitchen, he closed the door to muffle the sound and turned on the tap. He downed the glass of water greedily.

Then he retraced his steps, making a detour to retrieve his own phone, which was in his jacket pocket, before he stood there gazing at the sleeping figure. While he respected her decision not to have further surgery he wondered if there wasn't another way to help her…a way that would leave her free of nightmares about people pointing at her.

A sense of deep grinding impotence rose up inside him. There *had* to be a way to protect her from all the cruelty out there, the people prepared to gossip and mock.

Chloe woke up and wondered why she felt so good, then she remembered and she felt even better. Eyes still closed, she patted the bed beside her, realising that the sheets were almost as cold as the sudden tightness behind her breastbone. Nik had left her again.

*No, Chloe, this is how paranoia starts.*

'Good morning.' Nik must have been back to his own room, as he was now wearing an unbuttoned shirt— a very good look on him—and cream linen shorts… Well, you couldn't have everything, she thought naughtily, knowing she preferred him naked. He was carrying a tray that held a cafetière of coffee, buttered toast and some fresh fruit.

'Hello.' She hid the sudden surge of paralysing shyness by grabbing for a piece of toast.

'Hello to you too. Black or white?' Nik asked, nudging the bedside lamp out of the way to balance the tray on the little side table. He sat down on the bed beside her and scanned her face.

She pushed a hank of hair from her eyes. 'Black and thank you, for earlier on.'

'I'd say it was a pleasure, but I hope that was perfectly obvious.'

She blushed, taking a sip of strong, fragrant coffee, and peeped at him over the rim. 'For me too.'

'I've been doing a bit of research online.' He was buzzing with the information he'd discovered and couldn't wait to share it with her.

She took another sip of coffee and thought ruefully that he had more energy than she did, as she felt tired in places she hadn't even known existed!

'I don't know who your consultant is but there is a team of medics in New York who are working on some new plastic surgery techniques. They're still at the trial stages but the results are nothing short of miraculous.'

She listened to him in silence but he had lost her after *your consultant.*

'I'm not interested.'

The coldness in her flat voice acted like cold water on his enthusiasm. He regarded her in frustration but when he spoke to her his tone was all gentle patience. 'I don't think you understand.'

She put down her cup and tightened her grip on the sheet she had gathered across her breasts. 'No, it's you who doesn't understand, Nik. It's you who hasn't been listening.' Or at least understanding. She felt a fool now for believing that he had. 'You really think there is anything you can tell me about possible treatments? Do you think I haven't looked into absolutely everything available?' She pushed her bare leg out from under the covers, shocking a small grimace from him. 'I've been living with this for a long time.'

He shook his head. 'I realise that—'

'Do you think I came to this decision lightly?' she asked him, her anger growing steadily. 'Do you think I didn't agonise over it? I came to a decision that is right for me and I need you to respect it.'

'Obviously, this is an emotional subject,' he began, 'but—'

Her lips tightened. 'Don't patronise me and don't try and change me. You need to accept me as I am, or walk away.'

He held his hands out flat in a pacifying gesture; this conversation was not going at all the way he had anticipated! 'There is no need to overreact.'

She arched a brow. 'No? Well, how would you feel if I brought you a cup of tea and told you all about the PTSD that you are suffering from?' She saw his flinch and ignored it. 'That I suddenly became an expert on your *problem*.' Her mouth tightened as her resentment rose.

'We are not talking about me.'

'Yeah, because unlike you I'm not in denial about my problem…and it isn't a problem for me. The only problem is the attitude of people like you!'

While she had been speaking the colour had gradually leaked from his face and by the time she'd finished his warm skin tone was ivory.

'I'm trying to help you!' he ground out, getting to his feet.

'How about helping yourself first? *I* don't need fixing. You're the one who won't even admit he has a problem!' she flung back, wanting to hurt him as much as he had her. A strange sense of calm settled over her as she looked up at him…this damaged, beautiful man she had grown to love in such a short space of time. This thing between them, whatever it was, had been doomed from the outset. It had never been going to work; she had only been fooling herself.

Why drag it out? she asked herself sadly.

'Until you sort yourself out… I don't want anything to do with you!'

# CHAPTER ELEVEN

SHE'D KNOWN THE event was being filmed live but Chloe hadn't expected the cameras to be outside as well.

She could hear the young woman speaking into the mic as she stepped out of the car that bore the royal crest of Vela. She squared her shoulders. If her sister, who absolutely hated being the centre of attention, could do this then so could she…all she had to do was channel her inner show-off.

'And this…yes, that is Lady Chloe Summerville, who is standing in for her sister, the future Queen of Vela. We understand,' the reporter continued with a coy smile for the camera, 'that the princess was unable to attend tonight, and, though there has been no *official* confirmation, I'm sure you recall how the Princess suffered terrible morning sickness during her first pregnancy…?

'Lady Chloe is wearing…' she consulted a sheet of paper she was holding '…yes, I believe she is wearing a creation by Tatiana… Lady Chloe, hello.'

Chloe paused in front of the mic that had been pushed into her face, and smiled. 'Hello.' The personal touch would have been nice but she didn't have a clue who the other woman was.

'That is a beautiful cape,' the reporter said, gazing

at the floor-length velvet fur-trimmed cape Chloe wore. 'Real fur?'

'No, it's not real.'

'You are presenting one of the awards tonight, I believe, to the little girl who, I'm sure our viewers will remember, ran back into a burning house to save her baby sister and was injured herself. Humbling...so humbling...'

'To *Kate*, yes, I got lucky being able to present that particular award.'

'Standing in for your lovely sister? And how is the princess?'

Sabrina was where she spent most evenings at the moment, hanging over a toilet bowl...still asking anyone who'd listen why they called it *morning* sickness.

'She is really sorry she couldn't be here as it's a cause very close to her heart. Heroes so often go unsung and it's good to redress the balance just a little.'

'So why was she—?' The fortuitous arrival of the cast of a famous reality TV programme saved Chloe from fielding any more questions, and as the camera moved to the new arrivals she made her way quickly up the steps and into the theatre's foyer, which was filled with small gaggles of well-dressed people chatting. Tatiana immediately peeled off from one of the nearer groups and came across to where Chloe stood.

Chloe bent to kiss her when almost immediately her phone began to bleep and, fishing it from the minuscule bag she carried, she glanced down. 'A text from Sabrina,' she explained, skimming the message her sister had sent her.

Good luck and chin up! If you change your mind that's fine either way. We'll be cheering you on, so have a glass of fizz for me! And hurry back, please. If my husband asks me if I'm all right one more time I might have to kill him.

Chloe's smile was tinged with wistfulness as she switched her phone off and slipped it back into her bag. What would it be like to have a man be as crazy about you as her brother-in-law was about her sister?

Swallowing the emotional lump in her throat, she knew how lucky she was to have a family like hers, who were aware of her plans and supported any choices she made. It had been a struggle to stop her parents from flying over to offer moral support, and she suspected they were a bit hurt by the rejection, but she knew it was something she had to do alone.

'Is everything all right?' Tatiana asked.

'Fine if you discount the fact that Sabrina can't keep anything down. The doctor says if things don't improve by the end of the week, they'll have to give her IV fluids.'

'Oh, the poor thing!'

'So what happens now?' Chloe asked.

'Well, you're up first so they want you to go straight backstage, and after you've presented the award you'll see Kate back to her table, where they've seated you there for the rest of the dinner.'

Chloe nodded. 'That sounds good.'

'You sure about this?'

'Quite sure.' Chloe was surprised by how calm she felt now the moment was almost here.

'You know there are going to be headlines.'

Chloe nodded again, refusing to give mind space to fear and doubts. Producing headlines was the idea. You couldn't challenge common perceptions from a position of fear. She'd been going around telling the world that they should accept people with scars while hiding her own.

Which made her a big fat hypocrite.

'Tonight is the night of the big reveal.'

'I think you're very brave,' Tatiana husked emotionally.

Chloe felt uncomfortable with the praise. 'No, the people being awarded tonight are brave.'

She'd never thought of herself as brave but she had thought that she had come to terms with her injury. However, watching a filmed conversation with the little girl she was due to present a bravery award to tonight had destroyed that particular illusion for Chloe.

'So what do your friends think about your scars, Kate?' the reporter had asked.

The little girl had put down the doll she was playing with and thought about it.

'Well, I think they thought my arm looked funny at first, and some kept staring. A few people, not my *proper* friends, were mean and made me cry, but everyone's used to it now, so they don't even notice it cos they see it every day and I'm still me.' She'd picked up the doll, applied a comb to its hair and added thoughtfully, 'I still cry sometimes cos I liked my arm the way it was.'

The hard-nosed reporter had had tears in his eyes as he'd wound up the segment and Chloe doubted anyone watching would not have been similarly affected.

She herself had wept gallons but her tears had been partly out of shame. She had been hiding, Chloe realised that now, and if she hadn't, if she'd been truly honest with herself and everyone else, that devastating scene with Nik a few weeks ago on Spetses would never have happened.

Now she'd have to live with the memory for ever, all because she had preferred to be treated like a woman with no imperfections. Of course, there had been a price to pay for her deceit: she'd fallen deeply in love. Flaws and all, she loved Nik Latkis, but he didn't love her in return. Unrequited love had seemed much more romantic when she was a teenager with a lurid imagination, but the reality actually sucked.

It didn't help that her youthful imagination was still hanging in there inventing implausible happy-ever-after scenarios, not that she was ever in any danger of identifying her fantasies as anything other than what they were.

It was the thought of Nik's far more sinister dreams that continued to haunt her. She wondered and worried about the demons that visited him in the night and the eventual toll they would take on his health, both emotional and physical. She longed to comfort him but knew that was never going to happen after what had happened between them. She didn't blame him for that; he'd tried, but her scars were obviously an issue for him and he wasn't interested in helping himself, either.

Would he be watching the awards ceremony?

Would he disapprove of her decision?

She knew full well that her big reveal would go viral on social media, sparking thousands of debates, which was good, and an equal number of cruel comments, which was not, from people who thought anonymity gave them the freedom to say vile things about people they had never met.

She was prepared for the impending blaze of publicity as much as it was possible to be prepared.

'Lady Chloe.' One of the organisers, an efficient-looking woman in a blue evening dress, appeared. 'You look lovely,' she gushed. 'Has Tatiana explained the format to you? Excellent. You really do look amazing. Oh, excuse me.' She stepped to one side as, at a nod from Chloe, Tatiana moved forward to remove her floor-length cape.

'It's OK,' Chloe whispered when the older woman hesitated.

Chloe smoothed down her hair, which tonight she was wearing gathered in a simple jewelled clasp at the base of her slender neck. Her dress was the same bold red as her lipstick, a silk sleeveless sheath cut high at the neck and low at the back, the reverse cowl open almost to her waist, and plain except for the pattern traced in hand-sewn beads along the daring slit that was cut high on the left side that fell open to reveal her thigh.

It wasn't accidental; she had asked Tatiana to do it that way.

'Stunning!' the woman began then stopped; she'd clearly reached the revealing slit. There was a pause before she lifted her eyes and during the slight hiatus Chloe fought the urge to twitch the fabric over the scars.

When the woman did finally speak, her voice was husky. 'That,' she said, looking at Chloe as though she were seeing her for the first time, 'is *beautiful*.' Then, clearing her throat, she waved away the assistant who had clearly been allocated to escort Chloe. 'I'll take Lady Chloe in myself.'

The lift was empty as they stepped in.

As the lift whooshed silently upwards the woman cleared her throat. 'My sister was born with a cleft palate and lip; it's fine now and you'd never know, but I remember the comments she'd get when my mum used to take her out in the pushchair. People can sometimes be very cruel and what you're doing is…good, very good. I'm Jane, by the way.'

Backstage was actually pretty crowded, but Jane found Chloe a seat in a corner that wasn't occupied by what seemed to be the entire cast of a hit West End musical, who were waiting to go out and do the opening number.

Jane left but returned almost straight away with a glass of wine, and stayed with her while the comedienne who was hosting the event introduced the musical stars.

'Your turn.'

Chloe jumped at the touch on her arm.

'Don't worry. Pretend the cameras aren't there.'

Chloe straightened her shoulders and walked out onto the stage.

Nik arrived late, but he was there. He entered the back of the hall and surveyed the tables that had replaced the normal seats in the auditorium, searching for his sister and niece. He had just located them and plotted a course towards them when a ripple of applause made him decide to hang back until there was a break in proceedings so he could slide unobtrusively into his seat and no doubt get an earful for being late.

Maybe he'd slip out to the bar…? He hated this sort of occasion and he'd have been much happier to just make an anonymous donation, but he'd been guilted into coming, not by his sister for once, but his niece, who had gone into Bambi-eyes mode and reminded him that he'd never taken her to the show he had promised for her birthday.

He was in no position to deny it, although he didn't remember the promise or the birthday, so here he was. He hadn't smelt a set-up, not until he heard Chloe's name announced, followed by another ripple of applause.

Nik only heard the name.

*Theos*, she looked magnificent!

Lust struck through his body as his glance moved from the woman standing on the stage to the larger image on the screen at the side of the stage. Elegant, assured, with the glamour of a siren of the bygone golden Hollywood era, she was wearing a dress that had to have sent every male temperature in the room sky-high… The thought of anonymous males lusting after her drew his brows into a straight line of disapproval above his eyes, but they relaxed when she began to speak.

A sigh of pleasure left his lips…he had missed that sound. The simple admission sent a shock through his body and he didn't catch what she said as he focused instead on the sound of her voice.

She had a beautiful voice; pleasingly low and clear, it filled the room. She must have said something amusing because there was a soft ripple of laughter…except he didn't feel like laughing. There was nothing humorous about the way he was feeling, the *things* he was feeling.

Did an alcoholic feel this way when they found the innocuous orange juice they'd just swallowed was laced with vodka?

What did they say about recovery? Something about the first step was accepting you had a problem…but what if you didn't want to recover—*ever*?

Frustration burned through him as he stood there staring at her, a multitude of clashing emotions swirling inside him. He desired her, he resented her…he had *missed* her.

He had been only trying to help her and she had thrown his actions back in his face, accusing him of being the one with the problem, assigning the worst possible motives to his actions.

Why should he defend himself to this woman?

The woman who had tapped into his deepest fears, the weaknesses he despised in himself, and exposed them all to the light, and she'd made it sound as though he had a choice…?

She was wrong. Knowing it was enough, challenging her mistakes would have made it seem as though he needed to defend his actions, or, as she saw it, his lack of action... Move on, she'd said, but where was he meant to move on to? He couldn't rewrite the past.

*A man takes responsibility for his own actions, Nicolaos.*

The memory of his father's comment surfaced, smoothing out the creases of uncertainty at the edge of his mind.

Strange how some memories stuck. How old had he been? He couldn't even remember what lie he'd told, or what childish rule he'd broken. Maybe the moment had stood out for him because it was outside the norm. His father had not had a hands-on parenting style; he had seemed as remote a figure as the portrait of his stern-looking great-grandfather that Nik always felt disapproved of him.

He remembered the shame he'd felt and the determination never to disappoint his father again; he'd be a man.

The idea that he hadn't lived by that adage ever since was ludicrous. As for feeling guilty about how he'd handled matters with Chloe, she was the one who had seduced him that night they'd met!

*Ah, poor you, the unwilling victim!*

His inner dialogue was interrupted by a sudden roar of applause, and Nik realised that he was the only person in the room still looking at the figure in red on the stage. The spotlight, along with everyone else, was focused instead on a table near the front.

The big screen showed a little girl with a woman kneeling beside her, obviously her mother, encouraging her to go up on stage to receive her award, but the little girl was shaking her head emphatically.

There was an awkward silence as the child began to sob loudly then, and it was a heart-rending sound.

He was relieved and pleasantly surprised by the show of sensitivity as the camera moved off her face. No, not sensitivity, he saw then, they were just following the story. It focused on the tall figure in red who was now walking down the steps of the stage.

A murmur of approval went round the room that faded to a silence as Chloe began to weave her way through the tables towards the child. A silence Nik didn't understand until he saw the image of her body on the screen. The camera had dropped to show the long legs, the daring slit and...everything inside him froze.

The lighting was harsh and the camera picked out every detail of the discoloured, twisted flesh.

*'Theos...!'* His stomach muscles clenched, not in reaction to the sight of the ugly marks, but the pain they represented, the *months* of pain they represented. The explosion of pride he felt drew a raw-sounding gasp from a place deep inside him he hadn't known existed. An emotion he had stubbornly refused to acknowledge.

Like everyone else he watched as she dropped down into a graceful crouch beside the little girl, the big screen showing her smile as she spoke.

There was another faint ripple of sound around the room when the little girl lifted her teary face from her mother's shoulder. Chloe nodded and pointed to her own leg.

The room held its collective breath as the child reached out and touched Chloe's leg, then released it on a sigh as the camera recorded the smile that bloomed on her face.

Chloe said something that made the kid laugh, then she got to her feet and held out her hand. The room erupted when the child took it, and together to the sound of applause they walked back up onto the stage.

Nik wasn't applauding, he was barely breathing... He

felt a maelstrom of pride, shame and an aching desire to run up there and take Chloe in his arms, but he knew that even if he had earned the right to do that, which he hadn't, this was her night.

As the tall, beautiful woman walked onto the stage and turned to face the audience they rose to a man and gave a foot-stamping ovation, which the excited child joined in with…and Nik knew he was looking at tomorrow's front-page headline.

He also knew he was looking at the love of his life.

And he'd blown it.

For once, no heads turned his way when Nik Latsis left the room.

# CHAPTER TWELVE

IT WAS NEARLY one in the morning when Chloe got back to her flat.

She rarely received a call on her landline these days, but the red light on her answer machine was flashing, showing her it was full of messages.

She ignored it, as she had already spoken to everyone who mattered, and her mobile phone lay switched off in her bag. She massaged her temples with her fingers to alleviate the tension she could feel gathering behind her eyes.

She could feel the exhaustion bearing down on her like a lead weight, but her mind remained active, not in a productive, problem-solving way, but more of a febrile, hamster-on-a-wheel way.

She kicked off her heels, conscious of a sense of anticlimax. She had been building up to tonight for days, not quite admitting how nervous she was about it, and now it was over and it couldn't have gone better, she should be feeling elated. But instead she felt…oddly flat, and not at all the inspiring figure that people had lined up to tell her she was this evening.

Easing the beautiful cape off her shoulders, she walked through to her bedroom, where she hung it on a hanger before covering it in a protective bag. Hopefully a few people would bid for it at the charity auction her sister had planned for next month.

When Chloe had suggested the timing might not be good for Sabrina to organise an auction, she had quipped, 'Trust me, I'm a doctor. I'll be feeling fine by then.'

As she stripped off the beautiful red gown and ran a bath for herself, she debated having a nightcap, but on balance decided against it, worried it might compete with the champagne she'd drunk earlier that evening.

Lighting the scented candles around the bath, she eased herself into the sweet-smelling water and lay there drifting, feeling deliciously decadent. Slowly the tension began to ease out of her shoulders.

Then the doorbell rang.

Her eyes peered through the open bathroom doorway to the clock on her bedroom wall, and she squinted to make out the time. Who on earth could that be in the middle of the night?

Everyone had warned her to expect some press intrusion after tonight and she thought that was realistic but this was ridiculous. It was getting on for two a.m.!

She decided to ignore it.

But her late-night caller was not giving up, and Chloe lay there, teeth gritted as the tension climbed back into her shoulders. And then the answer to her earlier question popped into her head.

Who did knock on doors at this time of night? The police with bad news.

Leaping out of the water, her pulse racing in panic and still dripping wet, she fought her way into a thick towelling robe and ran to the front door, leaving a trail of wet footprints in her wake. By the time she reached the door her imagination was cranked up to full volume and she was on her fourth awful possible scenario!

Cinching the belt a little tighter, she checked the safety chain was fastened and, as an extra precaution, picked up a heavy pale wood Dala horse from the console table and opened the door a crack.

Her late-night callers weren't wearing uniform and it was one visitor, singular, although she couldn't make out who it was.

Caution replaced dread, though on the plus side if this was a homicidal maniac standing there the walls were very thin in the apartments. Someone would be bound to hear her being murdered, and hopefully report it to the police.

'My neighbour is a black belt in karate!' she called through the crack.

She could only see a sliver of the man standing outside her door in the communal hallway, but as he stepped closer the partial view was more than sufficient to make the colour in her face recede, leaving her dramatically pale, and then return as quickly, dusting her cheeks with rose pink as she stood there frozen.

Her first thought was that she had fallen asleep and this was a new version of her recurring dream. In all the other versions, Nik had been wearing black swimming shorts and nothing else, not a dinner jacket that hung open and a white dress shirt that was pulled open at the neck and seemed to have several buttons missing. There were the remains of a bow tie sticking out of his breast pocket too; he really did not look his usual immaculate self.

'Hello.'

This Nik, with dark shadows under his eyes and stubble on his chin, still looked more sexy than any man had a right to be.

'I need to lie down,' she mumbled, thinking, *And then I need to wake up!*

'Can I come in first?' His mild tone was at stark variance to the glitter in his eyes as he stared at her.

'I thought you were the police! I thought Sabrina had lost the baby or my mum had fallen and broken her hip, or my dad had—'

'Sorry I scared you.'

'You can't really be here because you don't know where I live. I moved.' She'd rented out her old place as part of the entire new change she had decided to adopt on her return from Greece.

'Then you should consider going ex-directory, you know.' He dragged a hand across his hair and sounded tired as he added gruffly, 'Let me in, Chloe, please.'

'All right.' It took her longer than it should to remove the chain. Her hands, she noticed, viewing the phenomenon with a strange out-of-body objectivity, were shaking violently.

Finally she released it.

She stepped back as Nik walked in; he was real after all. Dreams didn't smell this good, carrying with them the scent of outdoors underlain with a faint scent of whisky.

'Beware Greeks bearing gifts,' she murmured.

Especially tall, lean, gorgeous Greeks with pride etched onto every inch of a classically perfect profile and with explosive tension locked into every muscle.

He held out his empty hands and turned them over. 'I don't have any. I wasn't sure if you'd even let me in.'

'I wasn't sure you were real,' she countered huskily. Then, shaking her head to clear the static buzz, she tried to inject a little normality into what was a very surreal situation.

'Do you know what time it is?' She flicked back the

hair from her face, the soggy ends dusting her cheek with dots of moisture.

'I couldn't wait until morning,' he said simply.

Struggling to convey a calm she was a million miles from feeling, Chloe met his eyes. The combustible quality in his heavy-lidded stare dried her throat and made her heart thud harder against her ribcage. She cinched the belt even tighter, suddenly very conscious of the fact that she was naked underneath her robe.

'Why are you here, Nik…?' Her eyes fluttered wider. 'Has something happened to Tatiana… Eugenie…?'

'No, they're fine,' he soothed immediately.

Panic subsiding, Chloe let out a relieved little sigh and arched a brow, folding her arms in an unconsciously protective gesture over her chest as she asked again, 'So why are you here?'

'Why didn't you tell me…?' He stopped and spread his hands. 'Tonight, you… No, you don't have to tell me. I know I've got no right to encourage your confidence in me.' He was the last person she'd turn to for support.

'You saw it on television?'

'I was there,' he said heavily. The pride he had felt for what she'd done was still there but overlaying it now was apprehension for her future. For every voice raised in admiration there would be another writing crude, cruel insults, but he'd be there for her, regardless.

She refused to jump to conclusions. 'Where?'

'At the theatre, for the bravery awards.'

The muscles along his jaw tightened as he realised with a sudden startling insight what she really wanted. She didn't want to be protected from people; she wanted to be released to be the brave, beautiful heroine she was. She might make those who cared for her sick with worry on her behalf, but it was a price they'd have to pay.

Nik knew with a total certainty that he wanted to be one of them, even though the idea of anyone hurting her by word or action left a sour taste in his mouth, and rage in his heart.

All he could do was be there for her—if she'd let him.

'Oh.' What else could she say? 'You didn't stay around for the party, then.' Her attempt at levity fell flat in the face of his grim-featured non-reaction.

For a big man Nik moved very fast.

The weight of his body made her take a staggering step back as he framed her face with his hands and turned it up to him.

'It was the bravest thing I have ever seen,' he rasped in a throaty whisper. 'Can you ever forgive me? I don't want to change you, I swear, but I'll change who I am. I'll—'

'I like you the way you are…'

His kiss silenced her. When he finally lifted his head his forefinger replaced his lips. 'Let me speak without putting words in my mouth…' She nodded dazedly, and he took his finger away. 'Tonight I saw the bravest, most beautiful woman I know…do the bravest, most beautiful thing.'

Her eyelids lowered over the haze of tears that shimmered in the swimming azure depths. 'I was scared stiff,' she admitted. 'I thought you'd be angry with me.'

The expression drawn on his chiselled face was one of astonished incredulity. 'I *am* angry.'

Her head began to lower but he placed a finger under her chin and drew her face inexorably up to his. 'But not with you, *agape mou*. Never with you. I'm furious with *myself* for wasting so much time!' he rasped out throatily. 'I know I have a problem with PTSD, and I'll get help for that. I might never be the man you deserve but, so help me, I'll do whatever it takes, so long as you take me back?'

She blinked in shock as she stared at him. 'Did I ever really have you?'

The shaky laugh dragged from her throat cut off abruptly as she encountered the hard, hungry, slightly unfocused look in his stare.

'From that first moment I met you, I think, but I was too stupid, too much of a stubborn, proud fool to realise it.' He dragged a hand through his hair. 'I really don't have any pride left, Chloe, and there hasn't been a day gone by since that morning in Greece that I haven't hated myself for making you think I was ashamed of your scars.'

She put up a hand and cupped his cheek. 'I see now that wasn't the case.'

'It's *my* scars I'm ashamed of,' he admitted heavily. 'Everything you said to me that morning was absolutely right. I knew it then, but I just couldn't admit it. Now I'm asking you to take me, Chloe, scars and all, for better or for worse… I love you, *agape mou*, and I need you.'

He took a deep shuddering breath. 'I know I walked away from you—twice—but I promise that will not happen ever again. Let me into your life and I will always let you be you. I don't want to stifle you. I want to watch you fly.'

With a little sigh, she laid her head on his chest, her eyes squeezing shut as she felt his strong arms close around her. She stood there listening to the thud of his heartbeat, feeling the weeks of loneliness slip away.

Finally she lifted her head. 'I love you too, Nik.'

The kiss he gave her went on and on, his hungry passion leaving her feeling limp yet very happy when they finally came up for air.

She stroked his face lovingly. 'I feel as though a weight has been lifted from me the last few weeks.'

He took her face between his hands. 'I love you, I love every part of you, and, yes, I admit I did want you to reconsider the plastic surgery, but not,' he emphasised, 'for me. For you…'

'I realise that now,' she admitted.

'I don't know if you've fully considered this,' he began tentatively, 'but what you did tonight will make you the target of—'

'Internet trolls and other low-life, yes, I know.' She dismissed them with an impatient click of her fingers.

It took a few moments for the information to filter through to his brain…but when it did his hands fell from her face in astonishment.

'Of course I know that; I'd need to live on Mars not to know,' she said with a rueful smile.

'And you still did it.' He shook his head and gave a laugh. 'You really are the most incredible woman,' he declared with husky pride.

'Is there stuff out there already?'

He nodded.

'We're not going to read it,' she declared.

'I think that is a good move.'

He cleared his throat.

'Nik, why are you looking shifty?' she demanded.

Without a word he picked up his phone, scrolled down the screen and handed it to her. 'There are some other things out there you should probably know about.'

With a puzzled frown Chloe took it and began to read, her expression changing from bemusement to anger as she progressed. 'Oh, my God, who did this? Do you know who the source is? It has to be someone close to you to know all these details. It's a gross invasion of privacy!' she declared indignantly.

'Me!'

Her eyes flew wide. It made no sense. Nik was an intensely private person so why would he feed this story about himself to a journalist? 'I don't understand.'

'I gave this story, this evening. You made me so proud tonight, seeing how courageous you were, not hiding in any sense of the word... You were marvellous and it made me feel completely ashamed of myself. You were right: I've been hiding like a coward. Your name is going to be out there all over the media, and I knew I couldn't stop that, but I could show some solidarity so... I decided to join you and—who knows?—reading about what happened to me might even help someone else. I'm definitely going to do something about it, I promise you.'

'I know you will.'

'I wanted to prove to you that you could give me your heart and I would keep it safe and I am hoping that you would accept mine.'

Chloe's breath caught in her throat.

'And for the record I don't want to change a single thing about you.'

Tears pouring down her cheeks, Chloe flung herself at him, sobbing with sheer joy, and he swung her up into his arms.

Eyes locked on his, she took his hand and placed it on her heart. 'I know you'll keep it safe.'

*Three months later*

'Another builder has quit,' Nik said, wandering into the office where Chloe was working. 'At this rate we'll never move into the house on Spetses. You have to do something about her.'

'Me!' Chloe echoed. 'I don't think so. She is your grandmother.'

'She is counting nails! We are in the middle of multi-million-pound renovation of a classic sixteenth-century mansion and my grandmother is counting nails.'

'She is thrifty.'

'She is insane, and you know it.'

'She's *your* grandmother…' she reminded him, coming around the table and looping her arms around his neck. Nik kissed her hard.

'At this rate we're not going to be able to move in after the wedding.'

Chloe shrugged. 'I don't care if I start married life in a shoe box, so long as it's with you.'

'Now you tell me, after I've already had to cope with planning officers from hell, contractors who never answer their phones and, of course, let's not forget Yaya.'

'She's excited about us being her new neighbours… well, for some of the time.' Nik had not given up his London house.

'It will all be worth it in the end, you'll see, waking up to the smell of pines and the sound of the sea,' she said dreamily.

'So long as I can see you when I wake up, I don't care. Which reminds me, have you got the shortlist for the new team leader for the charity? I don't want my wife—'

Her eyes widened as she pressed a finger to his lips and looked over her shoulder. 'Hush! You'll give the game away! Imagine how upset everyone will be if they find out we already got married after they've been to so much trouble to arrange this massive wedding.' Somehow she didn't think that people would be that understanding about their impulsive elopement.

He looked at her, eyes glowing with pride and love. 'I couldn't wait to make you my wife. I just wish I saw more of you.'

'I know,' she admitted, stroking his cheek with a loving hand. 'But who knew that the charity would take off this way? We're interviewing for a team leader next week and there are some very strong candidates.' She squeezed his bicep and pretended to faint. 'Obviously not as strong as you, darling.'

Their kiss might have gone on longer if Nik's ninety-five-year-old grandmother, all four feet five of her, hadn't suddenly appeared. 'A man came who said he was a building inspector. In my day there were no such thing; we just build a house with no paper.'

'The good old days,' Nik murmured. 'So where is the building inspector, Yaya?'

'Gone. I told him my grandson and his woman were busy making babies, and if they weren't doing that, then they should be.' Chortling at her own joke, she shuffled out of the room.

'Well, they do say that with age comes wisdom.' Nik extended a hand towards the door through which his grandmother had just exited. 'How about it, wife? Do you fancy a little baby making?'

'Only if you lock the door. If Yaya walks in on us, I might be scarred for life…' As the unintentional play on words hit home she released a loud laugh.

Nik felt pride swell in his chest once more. His wife laughed when others might weep. She had a gift for living life to its utmost, and looking at the world through her eyes had finally brought him the peace he'd never thought he'd feel again.

'Have my children, Chloe.'

Her throat closed up with sheer happiness. 'It's a big house, Nik, and there are lots of bedrooms to fill.'

'So maybe we should get started.'

'You read my mind!'

\* \* \* \* \*

# MILLS & BOON

## Coming soon

BOUND TO THE
SICILIAN'S BED
Sharon Kendrick

Rocco was going to kiss her and after everything she'd just said, Nicole knew she needed to stop him. But suddenly she found herself governed by a much deeper need than preserving her sanity, or her pride. A need and a hunger which swept over her with the speed of a bush fire. As Rocco's shadowed face lowered towards her she found past and present fusing, so that for a disconcerting moment she forgot everything except the urgent hunger in her body. Because hadn't her Sicilian husband always been able to do this—to captivate her with the lightest touch and to tantalise her with that smouldering look of promise? And hadn't there been many nights since they'd separated when she'd woken up, still half fuddled with sleep, and found herself yearning for the taste of his lips on hers just one more time? And now she had it.

One more time.

She opened her mouth—though afterwards she would try to convince herself she'd been intending to resist him— but Rocco used the opportunity to fasten his mouth over hers in the most perfects of fits. And Nicole felt instantly helpless—caught up in the powerful snare of a sexual mastery which wiped out everything else. She gave a gasp of pleasure because it had been so long since she had done this.

Since they'd been apart Nicole had felt like a living statue—as if she were made from marble—as if the flesh and blood part of her were some kind of half-forgotten dream. Slowly but surely she had withdrawn from the sensual side of her nature, until she'd convinced herself she was dead and unfeeling inside. But here came Rocco to wake her dormant sexuality with nothing more than a single kiss. It was like some stupid fairy story. It was scary and powerful. She didn't *want* to want him, and yet . . .

She wanted him.

Her lips opened wider as his tongue slid inside her mouth—eagerly granting him that intimacy as if preparing the way for another. She began to shiver as his hands started to explore her—rediscovering her body with an impatient hunger, as if it were the first time he'd ever touched her.

'Nicole,' he said unevenly and she'd never heard him say her name like that before.

Her arms were locked behind his neck as again he circled his hips in unmistakable invitation and, somewhere in the back of her mind, Nicole could hear the small voice of reason imploring her to take control of the situation. It was urging her to pull back from him and call a halt to what they were doing. But once again she ignored it. Against the powerful tide of passion, that little voice was drowned out and she allowed pleasure to shimmer over her skin.

Continue reading
BOUND TO THE SICILIAN'S BED
Sharon Kendrick

*Available next month*
www.millsandboon.co.uk

# LET'S TALK
## Romance

For exclusive extracts, competitions
and special offers, find us online:

- facebook.com/millsandboon
- @millsandboonuk
- @millsandboon

Or get in touch on 0844 844 1351*

For all the latest titles coming soon, visit
millsandboon.co.uk/nextmonth